dar es salaam

dar es salaam

A NOVEL

Tara Kai

BRIDGE WORKS PUBLISHING COMPANY

Bridgehampton, New York

Published by Bridge Works Publishing Company,
Bridgehampton, New York,
a member of the Rowman & Littlefield Publishing Group.

Distributed in the United States by National Book Network, Lanham,
Maryland. For descriptions of this and other Bridge Works books,
visit the National Book Network website at www.nbnbooks.com.

FIRST EDITION

The characters and events in this book are fictitious. Any similarity
to actual persons, living or dead, is coincidental and not intended
by the author.

Library of Congress Cataloging-in-Publication Data

Kai, Tara
    Dar es Salaam : a novel / Tara Kai.—1st ed.
      p. cm.
    ISBN 1-882593-61-8 (hardcover : alk. paper)
    1. Dar es Salaam (Tanzania)—Fiction. 2. East
Indians—Tanzania—Fiction. 3. British—Tanzania—Fiction. 4. Middle
aged men—Fiction. 5. Teenage girls—Fiction. I. Title.
    PR9507.9.K35 D37   2002
    823'.92—dc21

                                                            2002002840
                10 9 8 7 6 5 4 3 2 1

♾™ The paper used in this publication meets the minimum
requirements of American National Standard for Information
Sciences—Permanence of Paper for Printed Library Materials,
ANSI/NISO Z39.48-1992.
Manufactured in the United States of America.

For Pam

Who notices little things
and
thinks the world is beautiful enough to give it a voice.

Acknowledgments

Thanks to Jessica Clark and Sangeeta Mehta for their stubborn support and generous time spent on editing and preparing the manuscript for submission. And to Barbara and Warren Phillips for their patience and guidance.

dar es salaam

Silhouettes

I am standing on the stairs of the New Africana restaurant eating fresh figs. At the bottom, my sister Mona looks shorter than she really is. She's so helpless, just staring up at the swelling moon—like a chick, with her head at an angle. It makes me want to go down the stairs and promise her that if I ever die, I will turn myself into an angel and sit on her right shoulder forever.

We are here in Dar es Salaam. One night before our flight, Mona and I stayed up late and listened to ABBA tapes. I told her I couldn't believe that we were going to Africa. She told me not to say Africa because Africa is a continent. People travel to a city, not to a whole continent. She said it sounds dumb to say you're going to Europe; you say you're going to Paris or Rome. When I told Ella in school I was going to Dar es Salaam for my summer holidays, she said, "Where?" I said, "A city in East Africa," so she would know I'm not dumb.

"Did you see Mr. Porter's hair move?" Mona says.

"I told you it was fake, didn't I?" I throw the fig stalk at the dark breeze. It falls somewhere on the sandy shells and disappears into the black of the Indian Ocean. Now that I'm really here in Tanzania, I want to explain to Mona that colors are sluggish when the moon hangs itself at night. It's the moon that makes the waves sound white and foamy. The smell comes from some faraway time. I can't imagine waves any other way. This is the way they should sound. I want to ask Mona if she hears the same noises or if she hears sounds differently. "Shame you can't take pictures of smells," I say, waiting for Mona to tell me that I'm talking rubbish again.

She looks up at the giant moon and says, "God, Mr. Porter has bad breath."

"He smells of peanuts and seaweed," I say.

Mona looks up at the sky as if, all this time, she is following a blue butterfly—it makes her look so exact. I put the palm of my hand on my hair and move it up and down mimicking Mr. Porter, "*I love your family.*" Mona turns to me and laughs. I keep his deep tone, "*You are a generous man, Mr. Livingson.*"

Yesterday, when we arrived at our rented villa, Jack invited this man, Mr. Porter, who lives next door, to my birthday party. Mr. Porter works for the American Consulate in Dar es Salaam.

"But Jack *is* generous," Mona says.

"Big deal."

"He loves you." Her "you" means no one else but me. I feel all warm and flaky inside. Not because Jack Livingson, my stepfather, is anyone special but because Mona sees that I am somebody.

"Jack is stupid and crude," I say like I don't care.

"He even loves you calling him 'stupid.'"

2

"You know," I whisper, "I told him to fuck off once and he didn't say anything."

"God, I could never say that." She looks at me and I try to guess if she is proud of me.

I can see the brittle outline of the others from here. They are sitting at the table at the restaurant. All the tables are crowded; the tanned Americans, Germans, and the red-skinned English and a few Indians have come out. Our table is oval and has pretty, round candles that make your face look pink and heated. Plates with the remains are cleared away by waiters wearing black pants and white, short-sleeved shirts that are a little too tight. The table that was in order at the beginning now just has wine glasses and used, tired cloth napkins on it. I like this place because the tables on the patio facing the ocean are symmetrical. From our table, you can see two palm trees that look like they were planted there on purpose. Everything is neat and tidy and the waiters slip in and out of their orderly routine like a magician's assistants.

Mona walks even when she is standing. She either moves a little to the left or right, or taps her feet or goes from one side of the stairs to the other. She hums a tune that I don't recognize. This means that she is bored or nervous. I wonder if she will think I'm bad when I tell her. But I want to tell her before we go back to our table. It's on the tip of my tongue. It'll just come out, pull the veil off its face and stand there naked. I have to tell it because then all the commotion in my stomach will stop and everything will make sense.

"Mona?"

"What?" She looks at me to see if I'm looking at her.

"Do you have any secrets?"

"Lots," she says.

"Tell me one."

"Secrets mean you don't tell."

"What's the point if you don't tell?" She looks like a drawing that someone has traced from a photograph. Her short, wavy brown hair is tucked behind her ears.

"People who tell aren't adults yet," she says with a swaying tone. "Secrets keep you safe. Remember that." She looks at me like she knows all my secrets.

Her shoulders are hunched as always, and she starts walking toward the restaurant where Jack, Mother, Peter and Mr. Porter are sitting. She must be following her butterfly.

"Look, I tell my secrets to you," I say, following her.

"You don't have anything interesting."

"Maybe I haven't told you yet."

Mona says, "Tell me and I'll tell you if it's any good."

"I'm not going to tell you."

"OK." She's only testing me to see if I can hold out.

Out there, Jack's voice and Mr. Porter's smoky laughter and the sound of forks against plates get louder when you're not really listening.

"Well, it has to do with some feelings." I want her to listen.

"Just say it." I open my mouth to talk but my throat swells and nothing comes out. "If you're not going to say, then I'm not, either."

"You'll tell me when you're ready." She reaches back and holds my hand and we walk toward the light on the tissuey sand, splitting crusty shells under our feet.

"If you stand long enough, you can pick out your shadow," I say. We let our eyes get used to the inky shapes of silhouette. Still shadows take up the shape of real things. My half-face on the wall is almost me—my wavy long hair parted on the side. Each time I turn to see myself, my shadow moves. Without moving my head, I turn my eyes as far as they go, but just a little turn and my shadow melts.

There's a shadow next to one of the palm trees. It moves and then it becomes two. The man-shadow has a hand on one side of a she-shadow neck. She has her head back. He's biting, no, kissing her neck, his hand goes inside her dress, on her breast, and he is holding her other hand down. I know Mona is going to see me stare but I'm stuck. The woman is breathing heavily and it makes me feel something down there. It aches; it's not a pain but it moves and it's OK.

Mona pulls me by the hand and I can tell she is embarrassed as if she's the woman-shadow by the tree and has been caught. She doesn't know that she isn't guilty because she hasn't done anything wrong. Mother had that same look when I woke up one night in London and felt her move Jack's arm from my belly. I had gotten into their bed, smelt the whisky on his breath, and had fallen asleep between them. She was embarrassed because I saw Jack's hairy body and his small thing under his swollen belly.

Jack's voice comes from the light and the silhouettes are gone. "Education is everything. Tatum there has brains," he points the glass with the reddish brown liquid toward me. "With her, you have to be careful." Then he points to my brother, Peter. "That lazy boy over there." Peter just raises his head long enough to show that he doesn't care. "He gets pampered by this woman." Jack puts his hand on Mother's lap. She bites her lower lip and looks away, embarrassed by his drunkenness. Mona just stands there and hums.

None of us belong to Jack. Mother is our mother and Dad is our father.

"Did you like your birthday dinner?" Mr. Porter asks me.

"Yes," I say.

"How old are you today?"

"Fourteen," says Jack. "She's big for her age." I know that if I stop eating I would be perfect. My breasts don't go with the rest of my body. The bra mother bought me last month feels like a stiff, choking rope around my chest.

"You are a decent man and you have a fantastic family," Mr. Porter says, his fake hair rolling with each syllable.

Jack says, "They are going to fall in love in this place."

"With this place," Mother corrects him.

"What?" Jack barely turns his head.

Her voice is low. "You missed out on school too much." She talks almost without sounds coming out of her mouth as if they are not great, not to anyone and not to herself. She collects the crumbs on the table like she always does; her hand pushes them into a heap and then picks them up and throws them in the plate.

"Dar es Salaam—they are going to love it," Jack says. Mona puts a large fresh fig on Peter's napkin. "Here, I kept this for you."

The Villa

Today is our third day in Africa. It sounds so funny, *Africa,*
a continent you learn about in school, a place an abiding
giraffe used to live in and now it's in the zoo. There are
jungles and satin snakes, Tarzan and black women
wrapped in peachy dresses when I think of Africa. Not the
sewer-smelling streets, hotels with miniature soaps or the
armored shops we saw as we drove from the airport.

Our rented villa in Dar es Salaam is huge. It's made of
white stone and plaster and looks like any other detached
house you see in pictures where there is a beach, then a
road, then a pretty house with a garden and gates all
around. If Mother had friends, she could have garden parties here. The loose gate separating the garden from the
road is made up of two simple horizontal wooden blocks
that turn the same direction as the road. The fences look
as if they are here to keep a herd of aimless sheep in the
garden, like the white fences in the fields in England. But
there are no sheep here. There are houses on either side.
The garden walls are too high to look over. The small pool

is in front of the house that faces the Indian Ocean. If you stand in front of the house, you would think that it has lots of rooms because there are twelve windows facing you. But it's a trick. Every room has two windows, and the big bedroom upstairs has three. It looks nothing like our dark, red-brick house in London. London means cold rain against my bedroom window, and Mother bringing me milky tea with digestive biscuits.

Jack told us that Mo is coming back from Arusha today—Mohammad is his real name. Ever since Mother married Jack seven years ago, he has been telling us about Mo. "I would trust him with my life," he would say, with an abrupt wave of his hand like he was on stage. He told us that Mo is forty years old and never married and that he has the heart of a holy man. Jack's parents lived in Dar es Salaam when Jack was young, and Mo must have floated in and out of their house then. Jack said that Mo was like his little brother. Later, when Mo went to college in London, he stayed with Jack and his family until he found his own flat.

Mother, Peter, Mona and I lie by the pool of the house by the beach. With my eyes closed, I imagine us like floury paste wrapped in sunshine. If a rolling pin fell from the sky and flattened us into a silky, elastic surface, we wouldn't spread out. We always sit close like clumps of dough clinging to one another.

I think about what Mo might look like. It's a game I play with myself when I think about a new person. I imagine their hair, what they might wear, their voice and their walk. Then, I give myself points for coming close to it when I see them. I think Mo is short, wears glasses and has his hair parted to the side like the Indian man who walked us through customs at the airport. He will have big hands and will talk with a heavy accent. He might even have a hunchback. But Mo *might* be dark and thin like Salim, Jack's other friend who picked us up at the airport. Salim was so thin I told Mona he looked like a daddy longlegs. When Salim met us at the airport, Mona sat next to him all the way here, so still that I thought she was talking to him in her head. Salim has huge eyes, and his powdery face stared at Mona from the moment she shook hands with him. He carried our suitcases upstairs, said that he would be back and then disappeared.

"Ritual rite of passage." Mother sits by the pool with her feet in the water. With her real voice, she reads from her magazine.

"Initiation," I say. She draws the pencil away from her teeth and writes in the word approvingly. Her back is bent uncomfortably and she tenses her neck reading her cross-word puzzle. Her glasses make her look dusty and old.

"Smile," Peter says holding a camera. Mother looks up and puts on her "photo smile," just a lowering of her head; her eyes look up at the camera and she smiles faintly. Tongue behind her teeth, she lets her lips open slowly. She can smile in every photo but never looks happy because the sides of her eyes look down—it's not her fault.

"I don't have enough blacks, I'll tell you," Mona says. She sets up the Mastermind game and covers the pins from me with her hands, looking at the water glowing in the pool.

"Parallel positioning." Mother doesn't ask; she just throws those words out in the air.

"Juxtaposition," I say.

Mona says, "One black, two whites."

The shady sound of thunder in the distance makes mother look up at the sky and then back at her magazine. The sky is half-lighted and the air is humid. We're not allowed to swim in the ocean without either Jack or Salim with us. If Dad were here, he would take me all the way out to the ocean and tell me not to be scared. There would be nothing under my feet and the water would get darker and scarier. Lying on my back and letting the waves come close to my toes, I would push myself up with my hands so that I could float and not go under. The salt would sting my nose and I would give out a scream if a big wave came. Then we would come back and he would play Mastermind with me. We played Mastermind together on the plane to New York once, and he won every time although he had never played it before. I know Dad thinks of me because his birthday cards always come on time.

The muffled song "I Will Survive" comes from Peter's headphone. It seems to be the only song he plays. He must have recorded it over and over again on one tape and he just plays that tape. Peter likes to lie down wherever he is. Maybe it's because of his leg. His left leg is shorter than the right one and he walks with a slight limp. I only notice it when people ask me why my brother limps, and I tell them that he got polio when he was small and reacted to the vaccine. Peter likes to wear sunglasses, too, and he takes the camera with him everywhere. Once in a while, he will look up and take photographs of us. My lips and cheeks are reflected in his sunglasses when he leans over to see the Mastermind colors behind Mona's hand. When I check my pins with Peter, he shakes his head slowly. I change the pins and then he nods.

"Three blacks, one white," Mona stares at me. I pretend to think, then she asks, "What's your trick?"

"No trick."

"Very impressive, Tatum." Mr. Porter's voice comes out of his nostrils with cigarette smoke. Mr. Porter smokes all the time and he looks like a man who likes to keep things forever.

The sky turns gray and dark. Large raindrops fall on Peter's sunglasses, on Mother's magazine and on Mr. Porter's cigarette. We grab our towels and bags, run inside the house and stand on the verandah. The water pours down in a flood and bounces on the ground before it gets absorbed back in. My T-shirt smells of sweat and the rain makes it stick to my skin.

The monsoon breeze brings a strong scent. In the half-light of the afternoon, I think I see a man-shadow walk by our fence. I think I can smell saffron. He opens the gate and enters the garden. Jack goes to him and they hug. This is Mo at last. I watch him walk confidently toward us.

"This is Mo," Jack says. Everyone shakes hands with him. He is not as slim as I thought. He has a thick, dark body. His lips are covered with a black mustache with gray streaks in it. He stands in the rain and lets the water run over his hair and face. I push away my hair and wipe away the rain from my smudged face. A strange stillness settles over me.

His voice is British with a slight hint of a soothing Indian accent. Then he shakes my hand heavily and says, "Tatum, what a pretty name." The blood rushes to my head and I blush as I watch him go into the house with Jack. I am sure I see him turn around and smile at me. Jack takes Mo into the house to show him around. I stand with the others on the verandah watching the vulnerable rain. Mr. Porter keeps on asking me questions where I either can say yes or no.

"So are you excited about safari?" he asks or "It's humid today, isn't it?" to which I say, "Yes." Maybe Mr. Porter doesn't want real answers and just likes to ask questions. He told us that his wife never knew that he smoked till the day she died. He never smoked in the house and she never suspected. Imagine keeping a secret and never telling.

Mr. Porter's nostrils exhale his cigarette smoke. "She's an intelligent young lady, isn't she?" he says, moving his head out of rhythm.

"Yes." Mother puts down her bag and magazine and straightens out her two-piece outfit, and she gives out such a long sigh you would think she was going to talk for a while, but she just says, "She is a walking encyclopedia." I know she is going to look at me now, so I turn my head away from her. "Her father always says she's going to be someone special."

"Who? Jack or Dad?" Mona doesn't look up from the pins she has been trying to save from the rain. I don't really care who we call "Father," but Mona says that we should never forget who our father is. We should call Jack by his name and call our father "Dad." I don't think Peter cares, either, but I never asked him.

Mona reminds me of order. "She is the sensible one," Mother always says, and I'm "the careless one." Maybe when we were born, Mother made up one sentence about each of us so that she could tell people about her children if they asked, hoping we would stay that way forever.

"*Jambo, Asante* and *Penda*," Mr. Porter says to me.

"Pardon?"

"*Jambo, Asante, Penda.*"

"*Jambo, Asante, Penda,*" I repeat after him.

"Hello, thank you and love. That's all you need in Swahili," he says. "You know *Swahili* means 'people of the coast'. It's from the time of the Arabs because *Sahel* means 'coast' in Arabic." We all nod, interested. Then he picks up a magazine and sits on one of the verandah chairs. He reads the first page immediately, not like other people who would flip the pages first. He reads and reads and then goes to the second page and reads on.

Jack turns the outside lights on; now I can see Mo's face clearly. He doesn't look as old as forty. He has no frown lines on his forehead like Mother or crow's-feet around his eyes like Jack.

"Feeling better, baby?" Jack asks. He doesn't call anyone else "baby," just me. On the plane, I had watched the dirt airstrip shining like a mirror from the rain. The sudden heat outside had suffocated me and I had to vomit right after I got off the plane.

"I'm better," I say.

Jack's round stomach sticks out in front of him. He walks like he is carrying a baby inside him; that's why I call him "fatso." His arms are tanned and I can see the flesh right above his pants and the hair around his belly button. Jack would never be able to fly a kite with his hard-boiled-egg stomach.

Peter starts telling Mo about the on-flight movie: "Two hours of one dog drooling and making a mess of every-thing, and you can't tell the stewardess to turn it off." My brother Peter doesn't really talk much. He seems to be shy because he speaks with his ear turned to your face. His eyes fix on a point right in front of him, and sometimes people don't hear him.

Jack tells Mr. Porter and Mo about our rented villa in his formal voice. He uses this voice when he thinks someone is smarter than he is. I don't know how he can tell but his other, deeper voice says things like "residence" or "invest-ment" or "insane" instead of "house," "money" or "crazy." It's funny because when I ask him why he talks so strange, he tells me you can't talk with everyone the same way, and I don't see why not.

There's a soft and light beauty in Mo's black eyes. Mo's hands don't look like anything I had imagined; they look like a blind man's hands.

"What's Salim going to do now that you're not frightened of driving?" Mona asks. Jack *is* scared of driving, but not in front of Mo and Mr. Porter.

"Frightened? No. I just don't have driving experience. Salim volunteered to do it. I can't do everything." Jack would never admit that he's scared of driving. He's scared of flying, too. He got so drunk on the airplane that he fell twice when trying to get up. Finally, he passed out until we reached Dar es Salaam. He's scared of dogs, too.

"We're going on safari tomorrow for a week," I tell Mr. Porter, whose fake hair isn't so unbearable after all. I wait for Mo to say something.

"Selous or Ruaha National Park?" Mo asks, fixing his sober eyes on me.

Jack says, "Salim is taking them to Selous."

When Mo gets up to leave, I stand up to shake hands with him. "My mother is on her own," he says to me, as if I know what he means. Why doesn't he stay with me a little longer?

"I'll see you all after safari," he says, and walks out, impenetrable against the pouring monsoon rain.

Safari

If someone asked me what color Africa is, I'd say it's like
dirt and red wine. Safari isn't anything like you see on TV.
On TV, you see animals from close up, and the voice in
the film whispers.

Here it is silent.

Just the engine and the sound of the wheels on the
scraggy road. Tall, scrawny, umbrella-like trees glare at
you. Like flat dishes, they wait for someone to come and
eat from them. The earth is mudlike; sometimes it's
chocolatey and sometimes it's dirty. The grass isn't how
you imagine grass to be. It's thorny and thick and looks
like hay. Brittle plants stick out of the ground for no reason. Everything is prickly—the bushes, the trees, the
grass, even the white flowers between the bushes you
know will hurt you. There's no water. Birds make noises
that sound like clattering pieces of metal.

My breasts hurt. I want to tell Mona the rest of my story.

We're lucky and see some monkeys cross the deserted
road. Their hips move slowly and steadily. A herd of zebras

are too far away for us to stop and watch. From afar they are slow dots surrounded by little clouds of dust moving in slow motion over the stripped, bare earth. We can't get close like a camera. I saw a picture of a zebra once, and its ears were like shallow mugs. I can't see the zebras' ears from here. They have their heads down on the dry grass and rocks. I wonder why they don't look up at the sky and see the clouds or watch the stars at night. Everything is flat and the grass is faded green and yellow. The heat smells and the dust and the long humming silence would strangle me if I were alone. The ground is swollen and scarred and nothing is soft or fluffy like the velvety pillows on my bed in London.

I watch Mother sleep in the front seat of the Jeep. She wears her faded sunglasses whenever she dozes off. Peter is sitting next to Mona listening to his Walkman. I like to call the van "Jeep" because it sounds more adventurous. I think about how we became a family. Did God arrange silky little figurines of Mother, Dad, Mona, Peter and I, fuse them together and say, "This will be one family"? Where did he get Jack from, and did he just take away Dad's figure when he left us?

We're on a road that only goes toward the split horizon. Our windows are dusty and a hot wind blows sand everywhere. I feel like there's only a half of me here. The one that hasn't washed in three days. I'm thirsty and hollow inside and wishing I were in the salty, green ocean.

Mona stares at Salim's profile from the backseat while he drives.

"What secret?" I whisper, looking out over to a dry river. I lay my head on Mona's lap. I want her to give sense to the confusion in my head and to tell me that everything will be all right.

"Whatever, just say it," Mona is waiting.

"We went to the fair one day with Dad and everyone, remember?" So many years ago we were one family. Family is only one thing—father, mother and children—one family. Like the Allens, a family. "Remember Mr. Allen and his wife and their daughters Beverly and Michelle, who came, too? And I sat next to Mr. Allen on the roller coaster?"

"What did he do?" Mona always doubts until you explain. For her, my funny stories from school are broken into her *watch out* warnings. By the time my story ends, the one about my friend who pulled at the flimsy wire gate to make a hole in it, it becomes a stupid girl who could have hurt herself. I take a deep breath. "I screamed on the ride. He put his arms around me on the roller coaster and . . ." Mona wants me to finish my story before she can caution me against men. I want to tell her my secret, so that I'll know what she thinks of me. What if she thinks I'm dirty? But I've seen the way she talks to Salim, so she must know.

Suddenly, there is a thump on the car and Mother jumps from her sleep. "What's going on?" Her voice is from another world far away. Orange and yellow fabrics, sounds and dark red elastic skin are all around us. A woman has holes in her earlobes so big I can put my whole fist through them. Her neck is heavy with necklaces full of beads in different shades of red. Statue-like faces stare at me. Their walks are like limbering dances. The woman bangs the door with a twisted stick that has belonged to her family for centuries. Her large eyes are moist and swan-feather white and she yells through her teeth. I see a man who looks just like her, bony and strong. Then another woman who could be her sister—I can't tell.

"I was just taking pictures." Peter puts the camera down. Salim talks to the red-painted man from the window. Someone strikes a heavy blow at the window by my side. Salim gives some money to the man and they speak a language so harmless, so soft that I don't want them to stop.

Salim says to Peter, "They say you stole their soul." They scatter, and with them go the spindly white cows with shiny polished horns. The small, round humps on the cows' backs shake as they move away and melt into the bushes.

"Will you now give me that camera, please?" Peter gives Mother the camera and we ride in silence. Salim turns to look at Mona.

Later, I look out the window after Mona has fallen asleep on my lap. It's twilight and the distant sounds of hyenas burst through the silence. It feels as if we're driving through someone's dream. Salim slows the car down and says that we are somewhere between Msanga and Kwangwazi. He points across the vastness at a dead mountain sitting in the middle of Selous game reserve that is larger than Switzerland. The sky isn't shiny; it's fading, fragile blue like old postcards. The waist-high grass holds the sunlight inside it until it flickers and fades inside the earth. It lets the heat out slowly in waves of short breaths. On a perfectly mowed beige pasture a lioness walks around a lion that is sitting. She flaps her tail at his face and tickles him. She makes undignified noises and the lion bellows at her, annoyed, his round belly swinging as he gets up and walks away. She throws herself on her back and opens her lower legs. "She's teasing him. She's in heat," Salim says. The lion gives out an earthquake roar. The thick mane surrounds his liquid brown eyes. He looks at something invisible, then walks toward it. The landscape is blotched with shadows of clouds as a trio of aloof giraffes moves in slow motion. Two elephants flap their ears in the warm air. They put their weight on the tracks that snakes and locusts have made on the salmon-colored sand.

The brilliant orange sun is setting and I want to wake Mona because she loves sunsets. Brown, purple and red melt and become slashes of gray-green. Violet light shines from somewhere far away and fades to the purest mute pink.

I don't wake her because the sunset is not complete. It will go on tomorrow. Colors you can't explain—maybe in a painting but not in a photograph. I watch this soft, pure and restful picture in silence. Click. Peter takes a picture.

Just as Salim had said, we arrive at the safari hotel late and cold. The crickets click in a chorus telling us that they are there. The darkness is shades of gray and red, never black. And the elephant there alone that doesn't seem to belong anywhere, just surrounded by nothing.

Purple

"Tatum has malaria. We're coming back tomorrow." Mona is on the phone with Jack. She wrinkles her forehead as she tries to concentrate. She holds her left ear while the Indian doctor talks to mother. I feel OK, just tired and hot. My muscles ache like I'm bruised and I want to sleep. I wonder if Mona knows that her nose is sweet and that her forehead is pretty.

The sweaty, shining doctor says, "Did you all take tablets four weeks before departure?" I don't want to laugh at his accent. Peter is in front of the TV changing stations. The headphones of his Walkman around his neck are absorbing "I Will Survive".

"I was OK this morning." My weak words circle around the green and black hotel room not getting heard.

"Yes, we all took them." For Mother everything is critical and nothing is a joke. Her face looks like an oval mask full of bad thoughts and worries.

"These things happen; it's mild," the liquid accent says.

The doctor is wearing a light purple shirt with splotches of orange, yellow, brown and black. I think maybe his mother gave it to him as a present. Maybe when Indians are born the first color they see is purple and they fall in love with it. Because everything they wear has the color purple in it. In London, those fresh from India have huge flower patterns on their shirts. Then, the longer they stay, the smaller the flowers become until, one day, they wear a plain white shirt and you know that now they belong.

"I've always said it. She's a sick girl," Peter says. I throw my pillow at him.

"Shut up, Quasimodo—I *am* sick." Peter holds his hands to his ears and says, "The bells, the bells."

The blood that the mosquito forced back into my body let trickles of memories from London into my head. Tatum is not here. She's in her room in London looking out at the rain, the cold and the dark gray colors that make her feel at home. I think of the time Mother had gone to work and I missed her. I went to her closet and looked at her dresses that had taken up her shape. I went deep inside the closet and inhaled the air around her. No mosquitoes there, no spreading heat that chokes you. And the sun, the bright, crumbling light that makes your eyes hurt.

I am burning.

Then I think of the red people. They have stripes on them in my dreams. Thorns and purple skies. I hear the purple-smeared doctor leaving. I lie on my back, my legs slightly open, and the red people quietly veil my face with silvery fabric and tell me to tell the truth. I say I want to know my feelings if Mother kills herself. Would I be ashamed? Would I cry? Would I clutch Ella's hand in school and want her to give me some real attention? I want to know; I know I shouldn't.

Mona wraps a blanket around me and cradles my head as she looks at my hands. Would she recognize them if my hands were cut off from my body? If she saw my severed feet somewhere, would she say, "Those are Tatum's feet; I recognize them."

"Tell me," she says. "Tell me your secret." Her voice crawls into my ear and stays there like lava, waiting to change.

"That day, on the roller coaster," I murmur. "I put my hand between Mr. Allen's thighs." I don't dare look at Mona. "He put his hand on my hand and moved my hand up and down."

Mona strokes my face. My skin is raw from safari. Then she takes my hand and brings it to her lips to kiss gently.

"That isn't a story. Tell me another one."

"I don't have another story."

I close my eyes and think of Mr. Allen's face—his eyes closed, sitting back and letting me put my hand there. It was Tatum who made him close his eyes. I was the one.

Mo

I slept all the way back to Dar es Salaam. I dreamt of the red, black and shiny lady birds I let walk over my fingers in our garden at home. One careless move, and they snap their wings and disappear.

I am lying on the couch in the villa with a grainy blanket over me that smells like sheep. The light hurts my eyes and I can hear their murmurs. What if I were deaf? No more sounds. Nothing. If I were deaf, when would there be silence? How would I know? The words on people's faces would have to go on paper. I would read people from bits and pieces of paper. "I'm Mo," he would write on paper. If I were deaf, there would be no more mistakes.

"She can go hiking some other time. Her fever is too high tonight." It's me Mother is whispering about. "What time are you leaving?" When Mother speaks, her splintered tongue pricks my skin.

"Early. I'll pick up Mona and Peter at six," Mo says. His commanding voice makes me tingle as it drips deep into my head and caresses me. A deaf Tatum would never have heard his unbroken words—like opening an envelope and finding a blank piece of paper with just the date on top and a signature at the bottom, leaving me guessing what words might have been written.

Jack says, "They want to go early and I have to get up with them?"

"Shhh. She's going to want to go, too." Mother is not talking about Mona. Mona, she loves. Mona is nice. Mother wouldn't be surprised if I put her in an old people's home, but Mona wouldn't do that. Mother got angry when I told her that she is only being nice to us so that when she gets old, we won't leave her.

"I got malaria a couple of years ago. During the day you're fine. The fever only comes at night," Mo says.

I look at him and my head is dizzy. His dark eyes look at me and say, "*Jambo.*"

"Hello," I say.

"Next week, when you're better, I'll take you with me."

Mo's heavy breath makes me want to ask him to kneel down next to me and spoon-feed me. I want to ask him if he likes ribbony lady birds like I do.

"Why don't you all go next week?" Jack asks.

"It's not a problem. I'll take Peter and Mona tomorrow and I'll take all three of them next week," Mo says.

"It'll be too much trouble," Mother says.

"No, I love kids. Besides, I don't have anything exciting happening in my life. Right, Jack?" Mo walks over to him and takes the beer bottle that Jack holds out.

"When are you going to have some excitement in your life, Mo?" Jack asks.

"I'm not an exciting guy. I don't even look for excitement; I'm too old." Mo looks down at me and puts his hand on my forehead. I raise my head to keep his hand on me.

"I'm not a *nfumu* but I think another week and she'll be all right," Mo says.

Mo's firm hand on my forehead makes me feel sunny. Then it holds my wrist. Gravity pulls me in. The fever isn't there anymore. It's the warm, humid air from the ocean that's making me feel like this.

"You'll be all right," he smiles at me.

There's an invisible snake moving inside me. It goes from the middle of my chest to my belly button. Between my legs I feel it. It's moving. I turn to my side and put my arm under my head. In my head, I follow the snake's moves inside, and watch Mo turn. I hear Jack talking to him.

This is what it must feel like when you fall in love. When you're in love, there are no more voices. Where do people's voices go once they're heard? Is there a huge bucket somewhere in the sky where they're all kept?

I watch them exhale hallucinatory words and then I fall into a deep sleep.

Seabird and Twilight

"God is perfect," they told me. Can God see when Mother hurts me? The hurt comes out so sudden, like the parsley aroma that sticks to the kitchen wall when Mother, knife in hand, cuts the leaves till they're just small pieces of what they used to be. She cuts me like that, too. Like the time she told me my skirt was too short and why did I have to show my thighs to all the men. Her words stabbed me in my throat and I felt dust in my mouth. I thought I would choke. Just like that, no advice or instructions. I remember hearing a train go by just as the words left her lips, and the sound made me feel safe, like I was locked up in a warm, dark shoe box.

Ella's mother would never have said such mean things because her mother is too pretty. Even at home, her mother looked dressed up to go to a party. She used to be an actress, but nowadays she gives sessions on elocution, the art of speaking. When I went to their house on something-upon-Thames for a visit, Ella's mother opened the door and looked through me. Her artificial curtains matched the colors of the sofa and she said to Ella, "Get your friend something to drink," and then, "You're the friend with that frightening high voice on my answering machine, right?" She put her hands on her ears and said, "Dear, try to speak in a deeper tone on my machine next time, will you?" After that, I hated Ella's mother more than my mother, because I was always "the friend" who didn't have a name. She was the mother who sent Ella to electrolysis. "Doesn't that hurt?" and Ella said, "Mother said when I'm grown up I don't have to worry about shaving." When I asked Ella why she doesn't stay over at our place, since I stay over at her place sometimes, she said, "Mother doesn't like me staying over, because she says you can never tell about people." Although I wasn't sure if we were the other people, I didn't want to go to her house again.

Now I don't think I mind when Mother's hair is messy in the morning or if she wears tattered clothes when she is at home. I don't even mind her telling me where each of the plants she has in our house in London comes from, which family brought it to us or where she cut off a small branch, put it in water until it gave off roots for her to plant. It doesn't bother me anymore that she can tell one fruit tree from another by the shape of their leaves. I can't hate Mother just because our curtains don't match the sofa. But I promise I will never nag when I marry; I will never complain like her.

This morning, after I had sneaked out with the others to go hiking, Mother must have been looking at a magazine, her head lowered, and she must have thrown sounds at Jack. I can just imagine her asking him, "You let her go hiking with them—just like that?"

27

"She didn't have a fever. She looked OK to me," Jack might have said, putting down his cutlery and pushing his plate away.

"God, you're a wimp." She would have collected her lips together and she would have been old again. With a voice that always scares me, Jack would have hollered back, "Shut up for God's sake. Just shut up, you stupid woman." I don't know if she really did scream, or if Jack called her stupid because I went hiking with Mo, Peter and Mona, while Mother was sleeping.

I didn't say much; I just walked behind them and was happy. So many questions were prepared for him, but when I saw Mo, the questions turned into silent vapors that came out the side of my eyes. What is Mother going to say when I get back? What could I say to her? Nothing I could say to her would make her less angry. "The fever was gone when I woke up," or "Mo helped me up the hill and smiled at me." It was entrancing walking up slopes, looking down on the ocean, the swaying of the palms, watching Mo walk, the heat, the humid air and the heavy load of the sun.

Clouds covered the sun when we reached the top of a spooky, black hill. Mo walked ahead, swatting busy flies away from him. We walked toward a cavelike space in the side of the hill. It was small and shrouded by vines and tropical plants. There was something alive but unnatural about it. Mo walked right in like it was the post office. Mona and I hesitated, a little scared, but Peter didn't seem to mind at all. In a dark corner of the gorge, a woman was squatting down as if she was peeing. She turned her head like a bird and smiled, revealing two missing front teeth. The large gold earrings she wore made her face look synthetic. An earth-color cloth was wrapped so high around her head that when she stood up, she had to balance herself with her hand.

Mo said in a whisper, "People around here call her the 'seer'. They say she can see things in the future." No one said anything. The seer walked deeper into her cave, and as if in a trance, we followed her, barely able to make out her fake shape in the darkness. The woman lighted a candle and the shadows of her tattered chair, faded red carpet, plants hanging down and her limping Dalmatian began to flicker. Freakish, orange and red drawings of cows and thin men with shields and swords dressed up the wall.

When she talked, it sounded like she was singing. Mo said it was Bantu. The seer motioned for us to sit down, so we all sat, cross-legged, on the red carpet. The turban on her head swayed as she rattled something in a tattered pouch. She opened the pouch, looked into it and told me to take something out. With my eyes closed, I slipped my hand into the pouch and waited for something to crawl up my hand or bite me. But I only felt hard, cool round objects. I picked just one; it was a multicolored marble. I gave one marble to the seer while she watched me closely. The woman looked at the marble under a candle, at Mo and then back at me. "Heartbreak," she said in English. She swiftly turned to Peter and offered him the pouch. Peter took a blue marble. Slowly, and with an illusive, motherly smile, she said, "All your pain will be rewarded one day." Mona got up to leave and neither of us asked her to stay. We all got up in silence and Mo gave her a $20 note. "That was it?" Peter asked. We followed Mona down the hill in silence. Once back at the villa, the hike and the seer began to feel fantastic, imagined, almost like it never happened, like a lie.

We go straight to the pool where Mother and Jack are sitting under an umbrella. She can hear us coming but she pretends to read. Jack turns and waves to us.

If I picture Mother as an animal, she is a seabird. She reminds me of one in a film I saw late one night about an old man. I loved the film but I never watched it to the end, because I fell asleep. Mother put me to bed and the blueness of the film became her. Once, on a boat, she said to Dad, "I don't think I'm the sea type; I'm the sky type." She *is* a seabird.

Mother doesn't turn to look at me. She says, "If you have fever tonight, you have yourself to blame." I don't think she can hide anything behind her face. She couldn't hide her anger when Dad left us the day that my cat Charlie died. When Charlie died, Mother drew her lips together so tight I thought they would bleed. Mona and I cried for Charlie that day. Dad wasn't there, so I don't know if he would have cried for Charlie, too.

Jack looks at me. "How do you feel?" He strokes my shoulder, leaving his hand just above my chest.

I take his coconut drink and sip from the straw. "Great."

I think death comes with a coconut drink; you take a sip to try and see what it's like. If you like it, you die. If not, you wake up and continue living. Mona says I shouldn't make death my main mission in life. It's not natural for me to think of tombstones with neon lights for myself now or wonder where angels are buried once they die. She says my head is always somewhere else and that I should live in the real world. If Mona were an animal, she would be a squirrel. But she's the older mother squirrel who doesn't fool around in the summer. She's the one that runs around and collects nuts to keep her safe through winter.

"She was a brave girl." I can't tell if Mo means me or Mona. He says, "They all were great." My face is all grubby and I know I smell. I don't want Mo to see me so close up; he can see my pimples and the hairs around my jawline.

Mo smells of undisturbed moss. His lips beneath the thick, quiet mustache are calm in the round and dark space of his face. Black hair grows with streaks of gray on his neck at the back. I hear parts of conversations because my mind wanders back to the silence that surrounded Mo when I walked next to him.

"Did my best buddy take you to the old woman seer?" Jack asks.

"She didn't say much." Mona says.

"People do their own interpretation of what she says." Mo's clear voice echoes in the air. "You know, like the horoscopes."

Hopeful flies play around in my stomach. Mo's peaceful, clear eyes under his bushy eyebrows move in slow motion. I stand right inside his bubble of silence and watch his every move.

"She only said 'heartbreak' to me," I say. I wonder if Mother has heard of this woman.

Mother wants to say something about me going hiking with a fever. So I take off my shoes and socks and start walking toward the ocean so I don't have to hear her. Mona follows me. Once we're far enough from the others, Mona says, "I'm going to remember this place for a long time."

"You think he remembers us?" I ask.

"Dad?"

"Yeah."

We reach the water and soak our feet in the miniature waves.

"Why shouldn't he?" Mona knows.

"Have you seen what we looked like five years ago?"

Mona says, "Ugly."

The sun's weight is on me, pushing me deeper into the sand.

"Did he tell you he loves you?" I ask.

"I don't know." She turns and starts walking back, looking at the clouds. White clouds were made for me. They are round and cozy on a brush of ivory and if I could collect anything to make me feel safe, I would collect creamy, fluffy clouds and put them in a jar, and every time I was angry or sad or scared I would let them out and touch them, and I would feel better again. Mona and I start walking back.

"That's right—everyone is stupid and you're the smart one." Mother's voice is pitiful when she speaks to Jack. Sometimes, when she's not around, I think I hear her voice. It seems to stay in the air long after she's gone. I think maybe when you are hurt, your body is sick and you take the hurt and give it to someone else so they hurt, too. Maybe that's all Mother is doing; she's giving her hurt to someone else so that she doesn't have to be the only one with the pain.

I'm glad I missed their fight.

"Remember the school choir?" Jack asks Mo in a tense voice, obviously changing the subject.

"Yes."

Mother starts packing her stuff to go back to the house. This stirs everyone else to start walking, too. She has to carry everything herself and "quick" is not quick enough, as if right now she has to go back to the house in no time. No lounging around, no looking around, just a straight path to the house. I walk back with Jack and Mo.

"How's my baby?" Jack says.

I say, "Don't call me that. I'm almost fifteen." I try not to smile.

"OK, honey-bunny."

"Stop it," I say, not really angry. I want Mo to see me like this.

"I'm sorry, cutie pie."

I ignore him and ask, "What does your name mean, Mr. Mo?"

"It's short for Mohammad. And Tatum?"

"It's short for ba-ba-ba-baby." Jack is being funny. I look at Mo to see if I can tell what he thinks of me.

"Say cheese." We turn to Peter and he takes a picture of me with Jack and Mo. The picture comes out of the front of the camera. One moment of time is frozen. The picture changes from brownish blue to red and orange, until it starts looking more like us. I liked the first colors better; they were more real. I put the picture between the book Mother has given me to carry for her.

Back at the house, washing away the dust, I wonder how the seer woman washes herself. I lie on my bed for a few minutes and look at the chalky ceiling listening to the mumble of voices downstairs. Twilight is my favorite time of the day. Crickets stop clicking for one instant and the warm earth waits for someone to light some candles. But it's the darkness everyone is waiting for, and slowly it makes an entrance. Mo would be twilight because he's perfect.

Jack would be the drunken bear who might lose his head once in a while and reach out and feel me.

Peter is the giraffe who doesn't want to be involved in things.

Mona is the unending, sober sea, and I am a white cloud who floats in and out of dreams.

Chickens

The bank teller windows are so small that they make you bend down and bow to speak. Mother does not look gracious when she changes her currency. She stoops down and speaks into the mouse hole in the glass, bowing down, almost begging the woman to give her money. If she could step out of her body now and watch from a distance, she would know. The shillings here remind me of history books, coins that are old and exotic, and the paper is too crisp to be real. Money here does not mean anything to me. Mother and I leave the bank and get in the Jeep with Jack. He's driving us to his dead brother's chicken farm.

"Chickens," says Jack as he drives the Jeep accurately—that's the word I would use—accurately. My favorite word right now is *exposures*. I like the sound of it. Mr. Porter was surprised that I knew the word *hibernation*.

We're driving through dense vegetation and Mother is sitting in the back, watching me. Jack drives slowly enough for me to see between the trees. The plants are deep green as if someone has tried to knit them together. It's hard to get used to just one pattern as the trees change shape and color as we drive by.

"A chicken farm in the middle of the jungle. Amazing how you can fool people," Jack says. He holds the steering wheel tightly and takes in a deep breath. Jack's profile doesn't have a solid, straight line. The eyes fuse into the nose, the cheeks melt into the mouth; it's not a face I could draw in art class.

"Maybe he liked chickens," I say.

"My brother only liked fried chicken, with chips."

"Will they kill them when you sell the farm?"

"Ray is dead and you're worried about the chickens?" Mother has to remind me that I say the wrong things at the wrong time.

Jack's brother, Ray, was twice as big as him. He was always eating and looked like he was lying down even though he was sitting. His face looked happy when you spoke to him. His sentences came out slowly because he had to breathe in air between words.

The day Ray died, Jack let out a little desperate yelp, almost like a puppy. I know because I was standing at the bottom of the stairs in our house in London when Jack came around the corner from the upstairs bedroom. He looked lost. He ran downstairs and said, "Tatum, Ray is dead. He's dead." Then he walked past me and sat on the sofa and turned on the TV, and looked at the screen hypnotized. Mother came out of the kitchen and didn't know about the phone call. She was making potato patties. Her hands were sticky with potato bits. She flattened the patties in one hand and asked, "What did he say?"

Ray was Jack's twin brother. Imagine hearing that you're dead. People who are unhappy are the ones who die. It doesn't make sense that happy people die.

Jack's family, as he puts it, were "part-time" residents in Dar es Salaam. Jack says that Ray was fooled into putting money in a chicken farm in the middle of nowhere. Mo must have known Ray. Did Mo give out a yelp when Ray died? Will Mo cry if I die?

We are at a clearing. There is a long, metal, rectangular shack with no windows. A few men greet Jack, as we get out of the car. I hear a humming; it's a chorus of voices. The sound is like a million birds singing. I walk through the two small iron doors and follow the sound that comes through a fog of dust. The yellow ground moves like a magic carpet. Chicks are everywhere. You can smell their waste and the metal taste in your mouth. Yellow chicks you can touch and kiss and hold against your face as much as you want. I pick one up and rub it against my face. It stares at me. Then it just stands in my hand and doesn't want to go down. It's so soft and fluffy.

"Take it if you like," Jack says coming in.

"I'll put it back in a minute," I say.

"You can't put it back in again. It'll die out of its incubation."

"Why didn't you say that before?"

"It won't live long. You have to take it."

I hold it in my hand and go back to the car. "Tell Mum I'm going to keep it."

All the way back, I wait for Mother to say something, anything. When she is quiet like this, I know something is wrong. I don't want to show her that I'm doing something wrong. I sit back and look at the yellow feathers, pink beak and the beady eyes and wish I could paint the chick.

"When I was young, I would look at the rows of cars on the road and wonder which car was the first on the road," Mother murmurs, looking out of the car window. "I never knew that there was never a first car. Same with people, really," she says almost to herself. Then she says, "I wonder if each generation is smarter than the previous one."

Mother thinks of things at the strangest moments. Jack is too tired to listen. I don't know what to say to her so the three of us ride back to the villa in silence.

MONA LOVES RAS. That's what the chick is called now—Ras. Mona says she can tell it's a clever chick. It doesn't want to move much, just stares. Mona loves animals; she used to have cute pictures of cats and dogs on her bedroom walls. Dainty pictures you see on birthday cards, and everything was light pink. Suddenly, one day, she bought different-color nail polish and makeup and put it on her vanity table. She took down all of her delicate pictures of dogs and cats and put them in a box. Now her room in London is all grown-up, beige with small strips of brown. Everything matches and is in symmetry. I'll never clear away my room from one day to the other. I'm going to keep my ABBA and Donna Summer posters forever.

I cover my bedroom with newspapers, so the chick can walk around. With aluminum foil on my hair and my ears sticking out, I tear off pages of a magazine to cover the bathroom floor.

"I want to marry a guy with long hair," I say to Mona, who's sitting on my bed. I look ugly now but *Cosmo* "beauty tips" said that for maximum effect, I should do the hair mask in foil for ten minutes.

"Why do you say such crazy things?" Mona says, stroking Ras's feathers.

I don't see why my thoughts don't count. I think them and say them, and she thinks I say dumb things. Like the time I told her I hate chocolate with wrappers that make a rustling noise, and that my friend Ella eats the top of the chocolate first and then licks the caramel away from the middle. I told her I don't think it's right for some strange man like Santa Claus to go to your bedroom at night to put things under your pillow. I'm not crazy because crazy people can't control what they think. Old people say things sometimes that don't make sense, but Jack says that's because they're senile. I think crazy people say the things they do because they're trying to tell us something from another world.

If I decided not to say anything one day, then Mona would think I was sulking. Nuns don't talk for years. I'm just going to write down things and pretend I'm talking to Mona. The first thing I'll write is going to be about three-way mirrors and that I can't see myself in them. Then I'll write that I like the sound that scissors make when I cut paper, or that I get hungry when I see dog food on TV. I'll write about the time I saw Auntie on her hands and knees under the table washing the kitchen floor with a cloth. She was the same aunt in the black-and-white photo, standing next to a thin man in her white wedding dress. Did she know in that white wedding dress that one day she would be on her hands and knees under the kitchen table? I'll even write that she doesn't know that her name in my address book shares the same page as some person she has never met. If Peter read my notebook, he would tease me forever. I could write about Mo. I could write sentences too close to each other so I can't tell what they were and then I'd have to make up the rest. If I connected all my thoughts from the notebook and made them into a story, I bet Mona would read it.

"You can't keep the chick in your room—you know that." Mona sounds like Mother.

"I know."

Mona is the one who gets me water when I'm thirsty at night. Once she kept her cookie all the way from school because she knew I liked cookies. She's the one I look at when Jack and Mother scream in the kitchen. If she isn't there, I look at the flower patterns on the tablecloth. Sometimes I just eat when they scream.

"Why does my hair look good just before I go to bed?" Mona says, looking at herself in the mirror.

"I feel like a nun," I say.

"What are you talking about?" Mona asks.

"I feel so warm and good—just like a nun."

"How do you know how nuns feel?"

I say, "They can feel themselves. Really just sit there and know what is inside them."

"I don't know." She doesn't say "rubbish" or "crazy". She just says, "I don't know."

"Who in this world would you want to interview if you could?" I ask her.

Mona looks outside the window and says, "The Virgin Mary."

She looks at me and I know why we both laugh.

"Would you ever kiss Salim?" I ask.

"Tatum, please," she says, annoyed. I look at her and I know she would kiss him any day.

Bathing Suit

If I wrote Mo a letter, what would he do with it? Would he glance at it, then leave it on his bedside table to shrivel up like an unused cloth in the humid air? Or would he fold it up neatly and put it under his clothes in his closet, and get up at night to read it again?

A week has passed and Jack has a new name for me, "chicken savior," because the chick isn't dead like he said it would be.

Ras, my chick, doesn't miss the yellow carpet where it came from. It greets me when I come in the room. I let it out in the garden and it comes right back to me and chirps until I stroke it. It isn't feeble anymore and it runs as if there never was a shed with thousands of other chicks to warm it. Ras is almost a complete chicken.

From my window I see Mo sitting still in a chair in the garden listening to Jack. Mo is how I imagine God to be. He isn't cut up in little pieces like everyone else. Not like Mother's eyes or Jack's lips, or Mona's delicate hands or Peter's ears. Mo is complete.

I am going to go downstairs. My mouth wants to say hello. He will see my profile and say "*jambo.*" Beautiful women don't really talk; they just stare into a space inside the clean, white walls of magazines. Maybe they have a gracious walk, and they must smell good. How does it feel to be one of the beautiful people?

I have to practice my walk, I think. I can't talk; that would ruin the picture.

My loose, wavy, dark brown hair has no pattern. In the mirror, my cheeks are too big and make my face look out of balance, almost blown up like a fish. I have Dad's eyes, not large or pretty. When I look at my eyes on the back of a spoon, I can't recognize them. I look as if I have been tortured. I look like a man with long hair. My broad shoulders and fleshy stomach I get from mother. If I just go downstairs and not talk, just listen and stare, maybe Mo will think that I have things on my mind and don't want to talk about them.

Jack says I have a nice body, and my friend once told me I had elegant hands. I want to be Olea, the woman in the book that mother gave me to carry and hasn't missed yet. Olea has short, straight, black hair, and everyone falls in love with her. She doesn't even have to say much. I want to be thirty-five, slim and elegant with a small black handbag and expensive perfume. Then Mo wouldn't be able to stop staring at me.

I only have one bathing suit. It's black and has white stripes down the sides. "Black makes you look thinner," Mother muttered when we went shopping for bathing suits. She stroked the elastic material and said, "People who sleep too much get big." I looked for a bathing suit for three months before I could find one that didn't make me look chubby. None of them could hold my body together. I wear them and I look as if my body parts have been glued together.

I choose the baggiest dress I have. It's quite thin and creamy. The clear cream I put on my lips doesn't taste of anything. The three-way mirror in my room shows that I'm lumpy. I don't like my profile. Sometimes, when I take a quick look at myself, I think I see mother. Mona says I even sit like mother with one foot curled against my calves. Maybe I should take a book to read or wear my sunglasses. I put on some Charlie perfume before I go downstairs.

Jack and Mo are sitting under an umbrella by the pool. "It shouldn't really matter; it's not about here." Jack points to his head. "It's about what you got here," pointing to his heart. He moves his hands as if his words are a jumble and he has to give them order. He talks like those men in old gangster films; his language is so simple with big hand movements that everyone can understand. Even his sentences sound as if he's memorized them from some film.

Mona's friend, Wykea, used to talk like that. She talked like the women in afternoon TV series. She would say things like "You know what I'm saying?" Mona says when her friend first came to London, she didn't go to language school. She stayed home and watched films and commercials; that's why she talks like that.

It's hot and clammy outside. The Walkman in my hand gives me balance. Jack watches me walk toward them as he eats his sandwich, taking one big bite and then two little bites to fill his mouth. I just don't want to be nervous and the earphones muffle the barking of dogs on the beach. They sound like they're inside a well wanting to get out. When I walk, my head bobs up and down and my shoulders are hunched. My walk must be serious like those walks women have in soap commercials. They are free. You can tell people by their walk. Mo's walk is dignified.

"Pretend you know what you're doing," I say to myself.

"Hello," says Mo.

"Hi," and I sit down at the table and turn my Donna Summer tape over. I pretend I'm looking for a special song. I press rewind, all the while looking at Mo through my dark glasses.

I'm breathing too fast. It feels as if my skin is evaporating. I stole a lipstick in a huge department store once and my skin dissolved—at least that's what it felt like. I looked around and put the lipstick in my pocket so slowly I thought I would faint. Now, my inner parts are wide awake and waiting. My center feels like powder and something is floating inside my skull. I look at Mo from the corner of my eye and try and push my jaw forward; I know I look better that way.

"Where's your chick?" Mo asks me. Jack has one finger in his mouth trying to get the sandwich pieces out from between his teeth.

"Oh, it's upstairs." I shouldn't say "oh" so often.

I am too loud, I think. I think of all the things I could be thinking of; these things quiet me. I think of what people might say if they saw me sitting here. They might go home and say, "Today I saw a girl sitting in the garden. . . ." But I can't think of what they would say next. I don't know.

I want to say words that have meaning for Mo.

"Someone in London is sitting somewhere and reading the newspaper." I say this over and over again in my head, because I know this one special thought calms me. This is what I think of when I walk in a room and I think people are looking at me. I just think of a person in London who doesn't even know that I exist. Usually it's a man, and no one in particular. I think of this man and think of things in detail, like what he's doing at that moment. This stops my nervousness. It takes me out of me.

Jack says, "You have to start thinking about what to do with the chick when we leave."

"Will you take him?" My mind is a mess. I shouldn't have asked that.

Mo says, "My mother might take it." He turns to Peter, who appears from nowhere and throws a Frisbee to Jack. "Over here." Jack catches it and then throws it back.

Mo is not tall at all, just a little taller than me. This is what a *stocky* body must look like. I read that word somewhere but didn't know what it meant. Stocky and full, that's his body.

"Going for a swim?" He sees the straps of my bathing suit under my dress. I'm not going to let him see me in my bathing suit. I would die.

"Maybe," and then my mouth says, "Do you want to come?" I panic. I shouldn't have asked that. It's too late now. I can't undo it. I can feel a pulse in my neck. I want to turn into a shadow.

He's so soft and perfect, how I imagine saints to be. I can't look at him.

Mo follows the Frisbee with his sensible eyes. I don't want him to see that I'm sweating. I follow his every move. I watch his eyes, his lips, his nose, his hair and his hands.

An eternity later he says, "I can't swim."

"What was that?"

"I can't swim." He looks ill at ease.

"Sure."

"It's the truth. I can't swim."

"Everyone can swim." It's a joke, I think.

"Not me. I never learned it." Obviously he doesn't want me to ask any more questions about swimming.

We watch Jack jump up to catch the Frisbee, his shorts almost falling down. I can see the line leading down to his bottom.

Mo doesn't say anything for a while and my head is too mixed up to think of what to say next. My daydream about swimming together in a beautiful blue lake and a little cabin disappears from my head.

"What does your father do?" I ask.

"He worked on construction sites all his life."

"What do you want to do?" Mo's question is so far away it doesn't make sense.

"When?" I ask.

"I mean what profession?" I can't tell if he's bored or he just wants to talk about nothing.

I always have an answer to this question ready because everyone has been asking us that since we were small. "Cameraman for nature films," I say, smelling the chlorine from the pool.

"Can a pretty camera-girl make films when a lion kills a cute animal?" He called me pretty. I try not to think about it too much. I will remember this forever.

"I won't do that. I'll film animals eating and sleeping."

"Good, very good." He has said this sentence one million times.

"Peter wants to be a conductor," I say. "He says he wants to stand there waving a stick at the orchestra and get paid for it."

Mo smiles as he watches Peter and Jack throw the Frisbee. He acts as if he didn't call me pretty.

Jack can't run; he hobbles fast and Peter's walk is crooked.

"Mo can't swim." I tell them so Mo won't know I like him.

"How did you get that out of him?" Jack is surprised. "He never tells anyone that."

The sound of buzzing flies in my head won't stop, and I have goosebumps all over my arms. My nipples get hard and I think, What if Mo sees them through my dress? There is a hissing noise coming from far away. Peter tells Mo not to worry and that he'll teach him how to swim in a week. He says if Jack can learn to drive, then Mo can learn to swim. And the rest is all disconnected and endless.

Hair and Dark Lilac

One day a man came to our school looking lost. He was the father of Nevin, one of the Turkish girls in our class. He stood in the corridor and tried to speak English to a teacher. Nevin stood there and stared at him; she looked like she had given up translating a long time ago. He fidgeted with his hands a little, turned and walked down the hall in the English silence that had made him speechless. I stood still in front of the classroom and couldn't help him. That night I had dreamt of Mother speaking with accents to me and I couldn't understand her.

At the lake, Peter and Mo float toward us. I keep quiet, like a porcelain doll that might break into tiny little pieces if she was moved. Coconut trees that move with the monsoon winds surround the lake. The fields behind the trees belong to villagers who moved to Dar es Salaam to look for work. Mo said they got it as part of an "*Ujaman*" policy, something like a socialist agriculture.

Hanging feebly to the splintery, plastic swim aid and paddling with his legs, Mo looks small and lost like Nevin's father. I wish I could swim over to him and hold on to his neck. Mona and I watch Peter swim in front of Mo. Peter says things like "Beat those legs." Peter always talks to people in a gentle way even when he is teasing. There's a lady bird drowning a few feet away, but I can't move my hand to save it.

I have decided not to eat anymore. I don't want Mo to see me so big in a bathing suit. On the float next to Mona, I lie in my rehearsed position, in a way where my stomach looks the flattest and my arms don't look so flabby. The sun is heavy on my face like a lantern that is being held right above my head. Through my sunglasses, I can watch Mo without him seeing my eyes. I turn around and lie on my tummy so that he doesn't see the front of my thighs.

Peter reaches the float first and lifts himself up on his arms. Peter's arms are skinny but strong. He has a broad chest that narrows down to a thin waist, something Mr. Porter praised last time we went swimming. "Tell me," he began his questioning. "Do you lift weights, Peter?" Peter only shrugged. Mr. Porter's questions don't get him anywhere but he keeps on asking.

Mo paddles his legs until he gets to the float and clumsily reaches for Peter's hand. I hold my breath. Water glistens on his body and the hair sticks to his skin and takes on strange forms. His breaths are quick and deep. I lie there hoping he doesn't see the ugliness between my thighs. The woman who waxed my legs yesterday said women shouldn't remove the hair around their bikini line because then they look like plucked chicken and men wouldn't like that. But Mother just looked disgusted and told her to do it anyway. I wish I had left my hair where it was. Mother said I looked like a baby monkey when I was born. Boys in school tease me in PE. They say things like

"Your legs have more hair than mine." It'll only grow back if I shave, so why should I do it for the boys? Mother said that it was too dark and too much and that it made me look dirty.

Peter looks down and says, "Not a pretty sight," meaning us, of course.

"Ignore him," Mona says.

Peter rolls Mona off the float into the water. She screams, "Idiot!" and splashes water at him. He looks down at her and she grabs his leg and he pretends to fall on her. Mona gets scared and goes under the water.

I haven't seen them play for a long time. They hardly ever talk with each other. I talk to Peter and I talk to Mona and we three talk together, but I can't remember them talking together or playing. Watching them play in the water makes me happy.

Mo is lying on his back with his eyes closed, breathing rhythmically. Sitting next to him like this, with my legs curled to my chest, makes me feel light and hazy. The day moves slowly like vapor. My sense of smell is so strong, I think I can smell the saltwater on him. Things seem to go through my head like a sieve. I piece together things I should say. Decades later I say, "Mo."

He says, "Yes?" If I wake up one day with him next to me, I want him to sound like this.

The humid air makes me want to choke. At last I say, "You shouldn't lie in the sun." Stupid, I'm so stupid. I shouldn't have said that.

"OK," he says sleepily. Mo seems anchored to the float as if he has been lying there for months.

His skin is light brown. He isn't thin or bony, but he's fleshy and strong. The pattern of hairs on his chest grows from his neck downward and circles around his breast.

The hair on his arms is soft-black and long, just like the hair on his stomach. I will dream about him.

I can dream anywhere. I can sit in the sun and make up stories of places I want to be and how it should look. Even smells I can imagine. In London, I could lie on the balcony and pretend I'm in Africa. Now, I can even pretend I'm in London. There really is no difference. In London I would pretend I was being filmed or was acting. Then I would read from a script and know what to say and wouldn't worry about who I am.

Tonight, in my bedroom, I'll pretend Mo is walking past my room and sees me lying there. He watches me. He comes in and strokes my hair and my face. He bends down and kisses me, but it doesn't go on. Here, he disappears. What else? Mother might come in. No, they have to be out of the house or, better, out of town. I'm at his house, maybe in his bed. My story has to tell me how I got there. I can't just be there. My daydreams have to make sense to the last detail. I make believe I have to stay because Jack told Mother I need to stay on my own to grow up. In my thoughts I stay with Mo for a week. Then I imagine I'm in his bed or in my bed when he comes to me. He touches me and tells me things.

On the raft, Mo's breathing comes easy and his stomach is strong and round. I lie on my back and watch his frame, his toes, and his elbow. A few millimeters and my fingers almost touch his arm. The smell of the sun and sweat slides across my body. One more move and I can feel him. I hold my arm against his and say, "Look how dark your skin is." A butterfly floats past my face and its colors become blurry.

"Umm," he says.

Metamorphosis is the word I like now.

"You're almost like chocolate." Food is in everything I say. Mo doesn't say anything. It's not me who's talking; it's somebody else in my body that has taken over and says the things I say. The real me is outside somewhere watching all this.

"Where's your father?" I ask.

He turns on his side and looks at me. He says, "He's gone."

"Oh, I'm sorry."

"I don't mean dead," he says turning on his back again. "He just left us. He came to me one night, kissed me good night, we hugged, and I knew I would never see him again."

"Do you miss him?"

"I was seven when he left."

The sky is pale and gloomy and there is the smell of burned ashes coming from somewhere.

"Why do you live here?"

"My family goes back decades." He sounds more confident now. "Indians aren't visitors; they've lived here generation after generation. Your father lives in New York?" he asks.

"Yes, with his wife." Why does he want to know about Dad?

"Are you angry at him?"

"No!" I say. "Why should I be?"

"Do you miss him?"

"Not really." I think a little. "We never really lived together."

"I grew up with my mother and my aunts, so I shouldn't really miss my father," he says. "I grew up in a family of women. My mother worked for a wealthy family. She used to clean and cook for them, and sometimes she would take me to their house and I would look at their house and their children's rooms and the toys they had." His eyes are still closed; he lies there like a king. I can imagine his lips under the mustache. They have a livery, dark lilac color. "I wasn't allowed to touch the toys," he continues. "They would bring out their toys and show them to me, but they would tell me I couldn't touch them." Mo pauses for a few minutes, then he says, "But I didn't want the toys, anyway. I've always been satisfied with what I have."

I can imagine his mother and aunts telling him how sweet and beautiful he is. "You're as gentle as an angel," they must have said, stroking his soft, black hair. They might have given him baths and fed him and told him that they loved him. What would they say if we got married? Would they say I was too young? I think of tradition and customs. "Would your mother want you to marry a virgin?" God, I am so stupid. Why did I say that? I shouldn't speak out my thoughts like that.

Mo's face turns pale; he sits up and says, "Where did that come from?" The stonelike air does not move, and the trees around the lake are paralyzed.

"I'm too old to get married now. No, they would do anything for me." He gives me a fatherly smile and I can see his dark lilac lips. Mo lies back and closes his eyes. This is the way I feel every summer—dark lilac.

"Women are strange. They always want something from you." I don't know if he is telling me this because I'm not a woman or because I am. "They want you to talk to them, to give them things, to touch them, to make them babies and to look after them." Mo sits up, sees a lady bird, reaches down into the water and takes it out. "And they can be manipulative and aggressive. My mother was never aggressive."

"Is that why you don't have a girlfriend?" I'm not scared to ask anymore.

"I love women," he says. "Maybe they don't like me."

I want to reach out and stroke his hair, his face and his lips. "I like you," I say quickly.

"I haven't seen one of these for a long time." Mo disregards what I said and looks at an insect climbing on the raft, and then he asks me, "Do you miss London?"

"Not really," I say. Maybe he wants to know why.

I want to tell him that I want to stay here. I don't want to go back.

"Why do you stay here?" I ask. I think of the next question fast.

"I don't want to be anywhere else. I get up in the morning, have my breakfast of bread and cheese and honey and sweet tea, then I go to work at the warehouse. It's just a short drive and it's still cool out." Mo talks like he is reading from a book. "I have lunch at noon and then go home in the evening, I shower, take a nap, read a little or go to someone's house. It's a good life and my mother is not alone in her old age." He's a powerful angel, the shadow that comes to me in my dreams. "I couldn't have stayed in London, and she would not have survived here on her own."

"Do you miss London?" I ask.

"I don't like big cities." He looks at the sun that is lowering itself behind the petrified trees. The moon is already out. "London was too cold and lonely. It was dark." I think of my dark room in London at night.

"Did you have fun with Jack in London?" I ask.

"Yeah." Mo leans back and smiles at his memories. "Jack wanted to set me up with someone." After a few minutes of silence, he says, "The women there were pale with thinning hair. They had transparent skin. And that Cockney accent—ah, how I hated that vicious accent. If only those women wouldn't talk."

"Do you want to go anywhere else?" We could go away together.

"Are you a detective or what?" he laughs. "I like my home. I like my routine," he says. We could stay home and he would cook for me.

"I wish I could stay here," I blurt out.

"And do what?" His chest looks so warm, so comfortable.

"Make films, take photos, learn Swahili." Say you'll teach me.

"Swahili?" he says, looking at Peter and Mona getting closer to the embankment.

"*Hujambo*," I say.

"*Sijambo, habari gani?*"

"I don't know anymore." Teach me, please.

Mo says, "But that was very good." He raises his hand and taps at the tip of my nose with his forefinger. I look down and smile. Then he does something that surprises me; he rubs the back of my hair with the palm of his hand. The water, the heat and his voice have made me drowsy.

"You're very pretty," he says. I don't know what to do. I feel like I'm in a movie and that someone is going to say "cut" and Mo will stand up and leave me. Maybe he did that with Mona, too.

"Thank you." I don't know why I said that. I saw a beautiful woman on TV who said she would make a big exit if she hadn't made a big entrance. It's going to get dark soon. I jump in the water quickly because this is a good time to make an exit, I think.

The milk-warm water calms my body. I stretch my limbs and float on my back, watching the sky. I want to be the color of sunset. Everyone loves sunsets. People stare at them; they're hypnotized. I don't know anyone who doesn't like sunsets. If I were the color of sunset, I would just stand there and let people stare. I can feel Mo watching me.

Oranges

Jack says I should be careful of cars and buses.

His friend, a cashew-haired American with thick almond-shaped glasses, is letting us drive his son's moped. At first, Peter said *he* wanted the moped, but when we told him he looked funny with his long springy legs, he said we could have it. Now I can drive it because Mona says she would rather sit at the back and watch people. She doesn't like to ride bicycles, either; she says bicycles are too thin and rigid to be safe. It's not that she's scared; she doesn't trust other people, she says. The moped is simple to drive. You put the ignition key in, press a button to turn on the engine, and then turn the gas handle and drive. Now we can even drive to town on our own and buy fruits.

There aren't many cars, but there are a lot of bicycles and a few buses. The buses are so full of people that the drivers can't drive fast. One bus drives slowly in a swirl of heat and black smoke, and anyone who walks fast enough can just jump on it. Men wearing murky-colored T-shirts and bell-bottoms hang out of the backs of buses with dazed looks on their faces. They are noiseless and stare out of the windows like rigid dolls. Peter told me I should take off my rings because people here cut off your fingers for them.

Our outings start with an idea. Mona thinks up a story like, "Imagine we have no money and are just drifting from city to city." We take a blanket and some things that travelers might take with them, like cans of food and bottles of water. I drive the moped to the beach, with Mona sitting behind me. Books we don't forget. Even drifters read books. I take Thomas Hardy's *Jude the Obscure* and Mona takes *Far from the Madding Crowd*. They're what we have to read for school when we get back. I read a book without looking at the picture on the back, because I don't want to see who wrote it. Writers never look like I imagined them to be. I can read and read words without seeing anything. I might think of clouds, the sun, the moon and the darkness. I could read two pages and think of nothing but the dark and how perfect it is and how I wouldn't mind dying if I knew I was going to feel the dark forever.

We find a shady spot on the warm sand, spread the blanket, take out our blood oranges and water and books. We sink into the soothing warm sand, too close to the seal skull and the skeleton of a wooden boat a few feet ahead of us. Mona and I don't really talk much; we just try to feel what it's like to be vagabonds. It's like acting. I have to feel it. I put thoughts that don't belong to me in my head and pretend they're mine. The drums in the distance beat with monsoon winds coming in from the ocean. I lie on the blanket and walk into Jude's world in Dar es Salaam. Once in a while, I look up from my book and see Mona daydreaming, maybe thinking of Salim. Salim opens the door for her, he gets her things, he looks into her eyes, he pats her shoulder, he talks to her, he sits next to her and all she does is move her head shyly away and smile. I want Mo to pay attention to me. I want him to look at me the way Salim looks at Mona.

It's twilight when we get back and I watch Mona carry the bags into the house. I think of Mo; I know where he works. When we were in the market, Jack showed Mother the gray metal building with no windows. Mother said she couldn't imagine working in a warehouse like that in the heat.

I know the way to the warehouse. If I go, Mother's angry words won't be enough after I've seen him. I don't want to think so fast. My heart beats so fast, it hurts my chest like I've swallowed a ruby. After Mona unloads the back of the moped and comes back out, I wave to her. "I'll be back in a minute." She looks at me from the rim of her discus-shaped sunglasses and wants to say something, but I drive away pretending I didn't see her. Thoughts dart by fast and I can't catch them; it's like when I wake up and remember my dream for one instant and then it's gone.

The roads here are bumpy and, in parts, not even asphalted. The mist, like a secret curtain, hangs in the air. Everything looks like it's going to be torn down next week. You would think the houses and aluminium structures were put together in a hurry with bits and pieces of material. Some buildings in town are made of concrete and are no higher than five or six floors. Single blocks of buildings stand alone. Waiting to be painted for years, but nobody comes to paint them.

When the women are out in the daytime, they wear baggy T-shirts over their skirts, and some wear dresses with zebra patterns all over. Red and orange and yellow and sometimes dark blue dresses with matching turbans move up and down the streets in waves. Maybe the women stay home in the evenings, because there are only men on the streets tonight. Men walk everywhere, whether it's on the sidewalk or in the middle of the street. They don't tuck their shirts in, and they seem to be one size too small and too tight. There aren't many people wearing real shoes; they wear sandals instead. Some men wear just trousers. Their top parts are naked, and they come back from work as if nothing is the matter. I even saw a man with no shirt but he was wearing a hat—all formal and serious.

There's a construction site on one side of the road surrounded by a fence. A crowd has gathered around a huge hole in the ground filled with people digging. There is straw all over the road. I have never been out this late by myself in Africa. The loud noise from machines, cars and buses makes me want to drive back to the villa. Around the hole, people stand frozen and hypnotized as if they've been standing there for years. Like colorful sleepwalkers from another world, the spectators stand close to each other, elbows touching, the folds of their clothes rubbing against the other.

I want to see the house Mo lives in, the stairs he climbs, the room he paces and the bed he sleeps in. I turn the corner into the warehouse parking lot, see his blue Honda and I wait. I park behind a car. It's now five to seven and I wait with the terror of not knowing what I'm doing.

After a while, I can make out that walk. Mo has a sweaty brown shirt hanging over his trousers and his shirt buttons are open. I don't move. I fix my eyes on his outline and see him cross the parking lot and get into his car. My heart beats so fast I can't move. There's an eruption in my stomach. I'm glad I have my helmet on. Mo can't even tell whether I'm a girl or a boy.

He drives slowly and straight on the main road. The other cars drive in a jumble. What if he knows I'm following him?

I don't want to lose him. There's a car between us, but I can still keep an eye on him and try to remember the way back at the same time.

At the traffic light, I see a woman with a long, thin, white silk blouse. She walks past the cars, turns and looks at me. I think, What a beautiful blouse. Then, she looks at me again; this time I see her eyes are vacant and her hair is messy and tangled. People turn and look at her and point. She looks crazed. I might walk the streets, crazed like her one day, wearing a tattered beautiful white blouse. What would Mo think of me then?

Mo drives for some time and then slows down. He parks the car around the corner from the main street on a quiet side street. There's a big mattress shop filled to the ceiling with mattresses. He gets out of the car and picks up his coat and a bag from the back of the car and goes through an old narrow door with bright shiny buttons. It's heavy and it squeaks as he opens it to go up the stairs. The building only has two floors. He lives above the mattress shop. I wait and gaze at the upstairs rooms. There is nothing. The curtain doesn't move, nothing. I wonder which one is his bedroom.

"*Machungwa haya ni thumni kila.*" The loud voice petrifies me. This language, the warm and humid air, the sound of the crickets in the dark and the round full moon make me come back to Africa.

An eggplant-colored man behind me has a large shallow basket full of blood oranges balanced on his head. With both hands he peels an orange with a sharp knife so fast I almost miss it. It is a perfect orange with so much juice I wouldn't know how to eat it. I don't want people to stare. I say, "No, *asante*," and get on my moped looking at him apologetically.

The heavy moon stares at me just like the lines on the street I lock my eyes on as I drive. It seems like hours that I follow the white lines. I drive through a narrow road that smells of foul coconut and sewers. A man, whose walk I recognize, goes into an old colonial house that looks like a miniature palace. It's Jack. I drive slower and wait till the beautifully carved doors, covered by a lotus and bold brass mountings, close behind him. I park the moped and, with my helmet still on, walk to one of the windows. The thick, red velvet curtains block my view. Behind my head, a woman's raspy voice says, "Come in and take a look." Her strong, sweet perfume terrifies me. What is Jack going to say when he sees me? What am I going to do? The woman has dark, wavy hair pulled up like a crown and her cheeks are so round and red, she looks like an opera queen. Her red dress has dainty lace around her collar and her wrists. She takes my hand and pulls me inside the wooden doors. My helmet is filled with loud music and laughter. I turn to run, but the lace-filled hand keeps me still. I look around in fear and can't see Jack anywhere. The marble entrance hall has a magic fountain in the middle, and in the back, I see some plasterboard cubicles with holes in them and I hear noises. Another woman with heavy makeup comes toward us and says something in Swahili. Beautiful black women sit on couches, scantily dressed with a dreamy look in their eyes, whispering secret words to each other.

"Are you a virgin?" the woman asks.

"Yes," I answer too quickly. My mouth is dry and I wish she would let go of my hand.

"How old are you?"

"Fifteen. I was just looking through the window," I offer without being asked.

"Do you like what you see?" her head motions to the women on the couch. An Indian man walks by staring at me.

"I want to go home." I hear a man's moans coming from the cubicle. It could be Jack, but I can't tell. A woman comes out of another cubicle. She is sweating and smudged and wears only transparent underwear. Her small breasts are erect and her body is perfect. I can't take my eyes off her.

"Go home. But come back whenever you want. I'll have a place ready for you." The opera queen's voice is so soothing and calm. She hands me a carved jewelry box with brass inlays and I take it, thinking she might not otherwise let me go. I know I will never come back to this place.

I ride back to the house away from the mattresses, the crickets, the oranges, the woman and the creaking bedsprings.

German

What would Jack do if I told him about the way that Indian man looked at me in the marble palace? I don't want to talk to Jack and I don't want him to look at me. I don't want to like Mo. I don't want Mother to show me that she cares. I don't want to think about Mo all day. I don't want Mother to fuss over me.

I do want Dad to tell me I should drink juice when I'm sick. I want him to make me soup and bring it upstairs.

"We are the only animals who dress up to have dinner," Mo says, pulling the chair to the table and looking around. The Moroni restaurant is full tonight. Women with round shoulderblades and wearing long black dresses sit at tables. Women with shiny, combed hair and painted fingernails walk in delicate sandals that are a little too high. Why aren't these women looking at Mo? Why don't they notice his confident walk, his strong voice and his hawklike eyes? Any minute now, I expect a woman to walk by and stare at him and ask him to go with her.

A man sitting at the table next to us looks like how I imagine a crazy writer to look. Like in a badly dubbed film, he moves his mouth and his voice comes out later. His two young daughters sit with him. They are so thin and so black and shiny, it makes me sad watching them. They are beautiful. Their tight tops and skirts match their shoes perfectly. Both shake out their napkins and pick up their cutlery one by one and wipe them. How did some girls come out so beautiful and well behaved? Who taught them all this, and how come they listened? They both sit upright, legs crossed, their feet moving rhythmically up and down although no music is playing. If it wasn't for their feet swinging, I would say they were perfect and dreamy girls.

I'm not dreamy or perfect. I don't like having a teaspoon with my teacup and saucer. I wonder if that counts as something good.

I watched a man and a woman in a café once. I turned my head, and when I looked back, I wasn't sure if they were the same couple. Either they were the same or they looked just like the couple before them. I wish I could leave lipstick marks on a cup when I drink so that people would know I was there. I wish I had a nicer handwriting, long and strong and thick so people would know that I'm not cut up in little pieces. It was strange. When the couple left the café, one cup had lipstick marks on it.

Even though she doesn't try, Mona has a dreamy look to her, too. But it's a dreamy acceptance. She doesn't say no, not to Mother, not to anyone. I don't just give up like her. She thinks they're always right, so she doesn't say anything. I know if I don't complain I don't get anything.

"The ceiling is moving," Mona makes us all look up at the roof of the restaurant. The slits in the middle move slowly away from each other. As the feeling opens, the stars force our chins to look up at them.

"The light we see from the stars is light-years in the past," Mo says, stretching his neck. "When we see the stars, we're looking at the past."

"I'm starving," I say.

I look up and feel warm hands over my eyes. "Make a wish." Mo's voice goes right through me. I keep the feeling and I don't want it to stop. I don't make a wish because I've known it by heart for so long, anyway.

"What was it?" he asks.

"I can't tell you," I grin. "It won't come true."

"All wishes come true if you want it bad enough," he says, like an angel from a Walt Disney film. If I were a director, I would cut to another scene where we're holding hands and kissing.

Mona looks at the menu and says, "If they don't, we should force them to come true." She is like that; she says things that she thinks are OK but they sound so odd. This she has from Mother and she doesn't even know it.

"Tatum's wishes all come true," Jack says. I imagine him kissing one of the shiny black women at the palace, touching her breasts and moaning like the men in the cubicles.

I try to give Jack one of those looks that Dad used to give us when he was angry. Jack looks away and laughs.

"She just killed you with that look," Peter warns him.

A small child runs past our table moving his arms up and down as if he has no control over it. Grown-ups don't move like that. Does that mean that the older I get, the more control I have? Does that mean that people will take me seriously? I will act serious tonight. I know Mo must be watching me.

As always, I order something and Mother asks me why I don't take something else, and then Jack tells me to try this other thing. They don't do it to Mona or Peter, only to me. I tell them I want to try the pizza and they say OK. Mother tells Jack what to order. He says he wants the steak and the waiter comes. Then Jack orders for all of us with comments attached to each order. Mo orders pasta with a salad and a beer.

"Tatum says she wants to learn Swahili," Jack tells Mo.

Jack talks as if I'm really his daughter. "She has an ear for languages. She took German in school." I try not to look at Jack. Did mother smell those women on him last night? Could she see red lipstick on his face?

"I know a little," Mo says. "*Auf wiedersehen,* and *ich liebe dich.*" It's like being on the highest point of the roller coaster, where in one moment, you know you're going to fall. It's the waiting that hurts, not the fall. Mo drinks his beer peacefully and talks to Jack. His jaw moves and he babbles on as if nothing has happened. He does not care. People fling things in the air without meaning. I shall talk only if it stands for something. It's the meaning that's important. Words can burn you. Maybe he's pretending he doesn't know he said "I love you" to me in German.

"Are there any prostitutes in Dar es Salaam?" I ask, looking at Jack.

"Tatum!" Mother says, looking apologetically at Mo. Jack just continues to drink his beer as if nothing has happened. He doesn't look at me, though.

The food comes and Mo starts to eat without waiting. He uses the small fork to eat his salad. He eats his food too quickly and even talks with food in his mouth. If I didn't love him, I don't think I would like his small hands.

The Clock

The clock on my bedside table says 0:00. Does that mean that time means nothing? I lie on my bed looking at the dark rain. When it rains in Africa, it's a thick veil, almost like a moving curtain made of mist and water, and it falls heavy. The dark room and the rain remind me of London. When I go back, will I be lying like this in bed thinking of Mo, or will I forget him? My room seems to get bigger in the dark. The clock now says 0:03. Three minutes past no time. I think I can even hear the clock ticking although I know these clocks don't tick.

I want a room that is mine forever. I would keep no furniture in it, just clocks showing zeros. The rooms in my head all face the ocean. I walk in slow motion. I might go inside every room and look out of the window and then look back in to make sure each room is empty. Not one piece of furniture, just wooden floors. All the doors are open. I would enter one room and look outside in the light and I would be happy. I would lie flat on my back on the wooden floor and close my eyes. My eyes are heavy and my head is empty and then I would die.

My left hand is on my tummy and my other hand is on my breast. My nipples are so hard they feel like licorice. I think it's the heat that makes me open my legs slightly and feel the sweat between my thighs. I touch myself down there and I think I'm wet because it's so hot. I close my eyes and picture him. Mo is standing in front of my bed, I have my back to him and he turns me around and kisses me on the mouth gently. I tell him no, but he doesn't stop. He unbuttons my shirt and touches my breast and kisses my body slowly. I touch myself down there. It doesn't tickle anymore; it aches. I forget to breathe. I give out a loud moan and I feel happy and empty at the same time. Mona can't hear me. The clock shows 0:27.

The Two Sikhs

This morning, before the sun came out in Dar es Salaam and started to make everything glow too bright, it was cold and breezy. Now it's burning my skin. Mother says she doesn't know why we came out at noon, but when she picked up her white triangle-shaped handbag, Mona and I knew we were going with her. She carried that handbag with her when she left Dad, just took our hands in hers and walked out of the house, with Mona running a little behind her and looking back at him accusingly. I don't remember exactly when Peter stopped coming with us on these outings. Did he just wake up one day and say to Mother, "I'm not coming"? I try but I don't remember exactly when he grew up. Now it would be strange if he did come with us, so we don't ask.

The market is dusty and hot. Mother said we won't be long and that we'll go to the Disney parlor for ice cream later.

I wouldn't call it a market because it doesn't have tables or booths; everything is done on the ground. Vendors pile pretty fruits or green vegetables on their gunny bags. No one sells more than two types of anything; some sell just one type of fruit. On the ground, with one knee up, a woman with brown marks around her lips sits behind her tomatoes and mangos and looks up at us. She has about fifteen tomatoes that she has arranged like a pyramid in front of her. Mother pays her for some tomatoes and we walk away. I turn back and the woman, like a witch with magical powers, has arranged the same pyramid in front of her.

The market is in an open area in front of two faded buildings with peeling yellow paint. The left side of the building has four small windows. On the right is a small but long balcony with rusted metal railings. There are yellowy sheets hanging out to dry and a small dim carpet hangs on the railing.

Some men are wearing what looks like small white squares of fabric that have been turned around on their heads. Mother says these are the Muslim men who wear wide, white shirts and trousers. Everywhere you look there are white caps. Most people stand in groups, talking or smoking. We seem to be the only ones buying anything. I don't have enough words for the different colors that are here.

Mother asks me what fruit I want, Mona looks and touches the fruits, making sure they are ripe or hard enough, and I turn my head to take in the hot air, smelling the metal and dust and chicken waste.

"How about this?" Mother holds up a straight-cut, handmade dress in the sun with a huge orange and red sun painted in the middle. Mona shakes her head.

A man's back a few feet away looks just like Mo's. It can't be him because there's a woman holding his arm. They walk away and he walks just like Mo. I squint in the sun and wipe the perspiration from my face. It's his walk; it's his back. My knees are giving way under me. I feel the air circling around me and I feel dizzy. I want to close my eyes and scream. I hate him.

I can hear Mother's voice. Mo doesn't see us. I want to be back in London—in our living room at night having Mother making me milky tea and bringing me biscuits.

"Hallo! We're going now. Ice cream," I hear Mona say to me. They haven't seen Mo and the woman. I turn and follow them in a dream. The woman's hair is long and shiny. She is Indian with a slim back and perfect calves. Maybe she smells of expensive perfume and has perfect white teeth.

Now I want to be a nun, dreamy and mute. If I could have white delicate hands and move silently like nuns do, then I would be happy. Why did he do this? What did she say to him that made him let her hold his arm?

The market is dark and gray when I follow them. Young black girls in dark blue uniforms with white collars burst out of a clay white building. They scream but nothing comes out of their mouths; all the noise is gone. A group of women block my view of Mo. They're dressed almost identically. They have made buns out of their hair, with golden round pins in them, and they all wear long flowery skirts. Some carry a plastic bag in their right hand and have a long bag draped sideways over their shoulder. There must be ten of them. Their language comes out with loud spurts of sound as if they're all saying, "Naaa."

I run through the maze of dusty colors and I think I see her hair and her slim back disappear in an alleyway. Suddenly, there's a strange silence, and like a door that opens by itself, the floor moves and I fall to the ground. The earth grows cold under my moist blood. I can smell the woman from the palace even before she touches me.

"This must be a sign," she says, helping me up. "Meeting twice like this."

"Didn't you hear me?" Mona's voice breaks as she tries to keep calm. "Are you crazy?" She's out of breath but manages to smile politely at the woman whose heavy makeup glows with beads of sweat. The woman takes out a lace handkerchief and wipes away the blood from my knee. This isn't the same woman who was with Mo. I look around for Mo and the woman with perfect calves.

"Put some ice on it when you get home," she smiles. "It's just a scratch." Mona and I watch her walk back into the crowded marketplace. When I see Mother, I start to cry.

"Let's get you some ice at the ice cream parlor."

Sitting at the bar, in front of the Walt Disney figures, Mother drinks her coffee while Mona eats her sundae. There's Goofy, and Donald, and Mickey and his dog, whose name I've forgotten. It doesn't matter, anyway. If it weren't for the man with leprosy in front of the shop, I would come here every day for the air conditioner and the huge sundaes.

"I'll order Goofy next time." Mona likes trying out new flavors. I don't know what mine is going to be.

Two men wearing small turbans sit at a table to my right. The two Sikhs could be brothers. Both are bulky, not fat but big. Their long, fuzzy beards come down to their chest. Their flowery brown silk shirts are tucked in their beige khaki pants. Even the color of their milkshakes matches their clothes and their chocolate-colored skin. They could be laughing loud but they're not. Just their bodies are loud. Shoulders moving up and down and head tilting to the back; they laugh in quiet rhythms.

There was a house in London with deep steps on which Mona and I would play. One afternoon, a car drove slowly past and a man stuck his head out of the window, staring. The Sikh's eyes remind me of that man. That afternoon, in front of that house, the man with the Sikh eyes shouted, "How much?" Mona made me turn and walk back up the stairs to where mother had been standing. When I saw Mother's face and Mona blushing, I knew what the man had meant.

One of the bulky Sikhs sees me staring and smiles. I turn and look at Mother's coffee cup. The other brother turns and stares at Mona.

"Your name," the Sikh says.

I hardly heard him say it, and Mona and I look at each other, unsure.

"Your name," he says louder.

I feel sick at having eaten too much ice cream.

"Beg your pardon?" Mother turns in her chair and notices them for the first time.

"Where you from?" the other brother asks.

"England," Mother answers him.

"Ah, England. London?"

"Yes," and she goes on drinking her coffee, a little uncomfortable.

He says, "Your name." As if that is going to explain things.

Mother looks at him straight in the eye and says, "It's not important." I can feel her discomfort. She knows they're not staring at her, but at us.

"I'm Bashir, and this is Kujri."

"Nice to meet you," she says seriously so that we know that this is the end of the conversation.

I don't want to be here. Men are stupid. They think we don't see. But I can see everything—the way they move in their chairs, the way they turn their shoulders slightly and put their hands to their chin tells you what they're like. The two Sikhs get up and leave. The parlor is empty and cool.

What do I say when I go back to London and school? Dar es Salaam is hot and dusty and there was a leper sitting outside the ice cream shop? There was a gigantic moon and I was in love with Mo?

The noise is loud out in the streets and the man outside with no fingers asks for money. "Shilling please, shilling please."

"How's your knee?" Mona asks.

"I wish it would rain," I say, trying not to limp. I don't want to be here.

As if reading my mind, Mona says. "You said you loved it here."

"I know." No one speaks. Outside, the cars go by and the heat throbs on my shoulders. I want to sleep.

That night I dreamed that the two Sikhs came knocking on my window. I opened the door. Outside in the dark, they waited for me to get on their magic carpet with them. I told them I had seen them once in my dreams before but they didn't believe me. Then it started to rain, first large drops, then it rained faster and faster, and the two Sikhs got angry and flew away.

Enza

Tatum on a piece of paper has no face, no hair, no skin. It's not me. It could be anyone's name. How many other people in this world are called Tatum? What are they like? Do their personalities match their crumbled names?

I write the name "Mo" on paper. His voice echoes around me, "*Ich liebe dich.*" Did he say this to that woman in the marketplace? Where did the woman come from? What does her voice sound like? Would she have lace around her wrists? What is the point of being pretty when this woman is there? Sadness stuffs itself into my mouth. It's the same feeling I had when I thought I was going to die from the atomic bomb. That was last year, when the teacher asked us to write something about the atom bomb. She said the Russians might press a button and then the Americans might do the same and we would all die. From that day on, I stopped doing my homework. When Mother asked me why I wasn't working, I told her that we were all going to die anyway, so what was the point. She shook her head and walked away saying, "Crazy girl."

After a week, when no one dropped any bombs and no one died, and the gloom had gone away, I started doing my homework again.

A few days ago, Mr. Porter asked if we were interested in meeting his seventeen-year-old nephew, Enzo, who's arriving this week. As if we're not going to see him anyway. Mona and I thought about what he might look like. Will he be skinny or fat or dark or light? Mona thinks he will be dumb and skinny.

"What if I pluck my eyebrows like this?" I show Mona a magazine I picked up from a store in town with pictures of Indian actors and actresses. The woman in the picture has long shiny hair and her lips are full and perfect. What is it that makes her beautiful—her skin, the black eyeliner, the lipstick or her perfect eyebrows? Mona puts down her book, looks at the picture, looks at me and says, "No."

Under the umbrella in the garden is a good place to read. I could read and read for days. My body is lying here in the garden, but the real me can just go into the book and not come back. Mona and I lie anywhere in the house, on beds, on sofas, on cushions or armchairs and read a book two, or maybe three times, if we like it. There was a book that I read at least three times. I can't remember the name. It was about a group of friends who went up in the clouds and found different worlds each time they went there. Another book had the word *Narnia* in it. Children went inside a closet and behind it was another world. What if I went into another world and everything was exactly the same? Only I would know it was different. Maybe that's what happens when people go crazy.

There's a slight breeze and a rustling sound. I lower my book and see Jesus Christ. He has long, slightly wavy dark brown hair and a goat's beard. His face is fine and bony as if he has lived a million years. His huge, blue hawkish eyes stare down at Mona and me.

"Is this your chick?" the voice says. Mona puts down her book and puts her hand across her brow to stop the sun from shining in her eyes.

"Yes," Mona says, squinting her eyes at Jesus. Ras, almost a full-grown hen, stops pecking at the warm grass and moves a little farther away, its cautious eyes looking back at us.

"Do you want to come over?" he says.

"Come over where?" Mona asks.

"To John's place," he says, motioning with his head to Mr. Porter's house. I never thought of Mr. Porter as John. Then he says, "You're Mona and Tatum Livingson."

We both nod. His fine fingers hang limp from his thin arms. He doesn't look nervous at all. A little shy maybe, but he doesn't fidget or anything.

"Are you Enzo?" My voice sounds faint.

"Yes," the wiry boy says, looking around at the garden. His voice is calm and grown-up, not squeaky like the boys in our class. "Who's who?" he points his finger first at Mona then at me. He has on a red T-shirt with a black image of Bob Marley, just like on the cover of *Zion Train*.

"I'm Mona." She's always so confident with people. Then she asks so direct, "What are you doing here?"

"Same thing as you."

"Why with him?" Mona can't seem to say Mr. Porter's name out loud.

"He's my uncle."

We both say, "Oh!" as if that makes more sense.

"It gets boring here, doesn't it?" He looks directly at me as if I have the answer.

"Safari's good," I say.

"This is Tatum," Mona introduces me, which he has figured out already.

"Take a picture," Enzo says, pointing at Mona's camera on the grass. He sits down on the grass next to me, puts his arms around my shoulder and looks at the camera. My mouth drops open in amazement and Mona takes a picture.

Nobody says anything for a while, then Mona gets up and says, "So," which means we're going now. I say to Enzo, "OK then, bye."

We walk back to the house and Mona starts doing her stretching movements. This is a sign that she wants to be alone. I stay and follow her moves.

"I think he likes you," Mona says, holding her foot, which she has just bent behind her. "Can you believe he just put his arms around you?"

"He's creepy."

"He's OK."

"Take him." I say this from memory, something I heard on a TV program.

"He's not my type."

"Right." She accuses me of not believing some things she says. I tell her it's so easy to lie, but it's really difficult telling the truth. She thinks I'm being smart.

Mona holds her elbow above her head and says, "Would you marry someone who wasn't your type?"

"What do you think?" I'm trying out Mr. Porter's habit of asking questions instead of answering them. It's a game, but it's better than just talking. I tried that with Mother, but she said I'm crazy and that I read too many books I shouldn't.

Mona has already guessed my answer. "I wouldn't, either. But Mother did." She means Jack.

"Why?"

"She told me he doesn't touch her," Mona says. In the quiet afternoon of Africa, I don't want to imagine Mother naked in bed with Jack and see him getting on top of her like men do in films.

I was maybe five or six. I woke up in the middle of the night and went to their bedroom. Dad wasn't in the room. The light was faint and I saw the pale, soft flesh of my mother's body. She lay there naked. Her hair was spread open on the pillow and she had a calm smile on her face. Her arms were not on her side, like how I imagined her to lie; they were above her head. She lay there so open, and her legs so slightly apart. I was shocked at her pubic hair, so dark and long. She looked at me and said, "Hi, dear, what's the matter?" She didn't move; she just lay there. She didn't try to cover herself or hide anything. I listened to the gargling noises coming from the bathroom. The light came round the corner and I remember thinking, If Dad comes out now and I see him naked, what am I going to do? The sound of the water running in the bathroom soothed me. I knew he was there.

"I can't sleep," I said.

"Go back to bed and close your eyes and think of a story. Then, tomorrow morning come and tell me. OK?" When I heard her soft, gentle voice I knew she was my mother and it felt good. I smiled and went back to my soft and cozy bed. I don't remember having that feeling again after that.

"She tells you that?" I ask.

"I didn't ask her to."

"Dad, I could understand. But Jack." I think, how could anyone want to marry him anyway?

"She couldn't stand Dad's other women."

"He doesn't really love us." I wait for her to contradict me.

"Dad looks after us, doesn't he?" She doesn't say that Dad loves me.

"Money isn't everything. Just because Dad pays for us doesn't mean anything."

"Dad loves you," she says it at last. "But he just doesn't say it." Jack tells us all the time.

"He wouldn't die if he said it," I roll my shoulders like Mona. "I don't know what Dad looks like anymore."

When I think of Dad, I think of a voice on the telephone. Then I think of all the things he might be doing while talking to me—watching TV, reading a magazine, kissing Jennifer, eating. It's always the same when he calls. We ask one another how we are and how school is, then he asks how Mona and Peter and Mother are doing, and then I ask him how Jenny is. Then I say, "Well, I'll talk to you soon," and give the phone to Mona. He doesn't know how I look, what my weight is, what size feet I have now, or if I can do a handstand or not. Mona always says you can't make people do what you want them to do.

"What do you think of Mo?" I ask her quickly, pretending I've just thought it up.

"He's old," she says. "But he's nice."

I watch the Indian Ocean and I am glad Mona is here to see it. I'm glad that she is my sister. Mona is the one who notices things and then shows them to me. "Look at that beautiful flower," she might say, and only then do I see the flower. Maybe I wouldn't see half of the things around me if she weren't there. What do people without sisters see?

At dusk, Mona and I listen for noises from our rooms that tell us something is going to happen, even if we don't know what. Mother in the shower and Jack in the bedroom half-dressed means we're going out somewhere. Jack is back from the chicken farm but it's quiet, so maybe we're staying home tonight.

Back in my room, I think of what I could do next. I don't want to read. Maybe I'll write in my diary. I hang up my clothes in the closet and straighten out the magazine, book, paper and pen on my desk. I like to form a line on my desk, where the paper's edge is in line with the table or the pen is parallel to the paper's side. It all looks so neat and has a pattern.

I still have Mother's book on my dresser. I started reading it that day at the beach when she and Jack were arguing. It's about a Frenchwoman, Olea, and all the men who are in love with her. She is slim and has short, straight dark hair and wears elegant clothes. She only loves one man, but that man is married to a blonde woman who is cold and heartless. The photo that Peter took of me, Jack and Mo is my bookmark now. The colors are more vivid than before and Mo's face looks more handsome. I look at his eyes that are not completely round. They're an elongated roundness. His eyelashes aren't thick but they are short and curly. His hands must be rough. I must remember to look at his hands next time. If I had money, I would buy him so many presents. I would buy him clothes and I would buy him a nice house and a car. I know girls shouldn't pay for boys, at least that's what Mona says, but I want to buy Mo everything.

I want to hear his voice, but what will I say when he picks up? I pick up the phone and dial the number that I have memorized. I'm excited. After two rings a woman's voice says, "Hello," then "Hello?" I hold my breath in and freeze. She is living with him. My hand hurts because I'm pressing the phone so hard to my ears, but I can't hang up. Then the door opens and Mona walks in. I quickly put the phone down and put the photograph inside the book where the first sentence of chapter 7 starts with "Flaunting is for birds of paradise . . ."

Kittens

When I ask Jack how many of us are going to Zanzibar, he says, "Isn't that the most beautiful name you've heard?" I want to know if Mo is going to come with us. "Zanzibar," he says. "It has such rhythm to it."

"So who's coming?" I ask.

"Porter's nephew." Jack doesn't use names like other people do. He says "the fat lady" although the woman's name is Miss Gee, and we have known her for years. Then there is "the policeman," although our neighbor in London is not a policeman, he's a security guard. So, for Jack, Enzo will always be "Porter's nephew."

There is the large island Zanzibar, and there is Pemba and fifty smaller islands off the east coast of Tanzania. In Zanzibar, the buildings are crumbling coral stone, and we're surprised when we see people coming out of buildings that look like ancient ruins.

On the first day, Mother stays at the hotel and tells Jack to take us to Stone Town. Walking through the narrow, twisting streets of Stone Town, you can peek inside open doors, push aside red curtains that hang where carved doors had once been. Inside, there are cool courtyards where sunlight has just begun to warm the latticework of balconies above. Dark cavelike rooms that lead to still more rooms surround the courtyards. Veiled women come out of some rooms followed by echoes of children's voices. I imagine faint lights throwing shadows on colorful rugs and ornaments and old, wooden side tables. Just like Aladdin's cave.

Peter tells me that Zanzibar is the first island that the Portuguese explorers discovered. We walk by the market and see hundreds of different spices and fruits; there's coffee and ginger and sugarcane and pepper and cloves. Mr. Porter told us that this man called Seyyid Said Bin Sultan ruled Zanzibar and made it into a wealthy country by selling cloves to the rest of the world. The same cloves that Mother sometimes puts into her "Indian" curries. They taste fresh when you bite into them, but then there's a bitterness that sticks to the top of your gums and goes through your nostrils. How can you get wealthy with cloves? Peter says the market is haunted by the ghosts of slaves who were sold here by the Arabs. Then came the Portuguese, then the Germans and then the British.

We are staying at the only big hotel on the island. It's huge and dark and looks like a castle, although it isn't. The hallways have dark red carpets and it's scary to walk there at night.

"The only hotel in Zanzibar and the only one that is haunted," Peter says. Mona, Peter, Enzo and I walk back from dinner to go to our rooms. Mona has been quiet all evening. I think she misses Salim.

"The waiter didn't say that," she says.

"What do you think *jinns* are—fairies? It means 'ghosts.'" As usual, Peter exaggerates. He puts his left arm on my shoulder slowly. I cringe and push down his arm. With him, you have to keep quiet so he doesn't know that you're scared. Otherwise he'll go on forever.

Enzo walks in front of us. "They're not scared," he says to Peter.

Peter grabs both my sides in the dark and says, "Boo!" so loud that even Enzo stops in his tracks and turns around. I almost want to cry but I don't. I think over and over that Mo is there standing next to me and holding me. I open the door to our room and go in.

"She'll have nightmares," Mona whispers to Peter.

She follows me in, shuts the door loud and locks it. I can't imagine Mona ever needing me.

I don't want to remember what the man said tonight, that *jinns* sit at the bottom of your bed and stare at you, otherwise I won't be able to let my feet come out under the covers in my bed tonight without seeing some shadow that might touch them. I don't like the dark, especially when there is a mirror in the room, because you see other things in it. The first time I looked in the mirror in the dark was when I bled. The first time I bled, I looked in the mirror and said, "You're disgusting; you're disgusting; you're dirty." I tried to forget the blood. It wasn't red like the red I saw once in a street parade on a Danish flag cut through with the white of a shifted cross. It was brown with a hint of red to remind me that this is really my insides coming out.

After class, in school sometimes, I would write "ALUCARD" on the blackboard when all the girls had gone. I would stand there and stare at the word in the empty classroom. I would pretend it was a word puzzle, but it was me who had written the word, so I knew what it was backward. I would say ALUCARD over and over again to stop myself from reading anything else. It would stop me from being scared. Now when I think back, I didn't have to scare myself like that, but I did and I don't know why.

Tonight, with Mona sleeping in the bed next to me in the hotel, I'm not scared of Dracula anymore, but maybe *jinns* do exist. I want to hear my own voice.

"Mona."

"Yes."

"I can't sleep."

"Don't think."

"I can't," I say. "Why didn't Red Riding Hood marry the hunter at the end?"

"Because she's just a little girl," Mona says. "Can't you think of nicer things?"

"Like what?"

Mona says, "Kittens."

"I saw him with a woman in the market," I say.

"I know."

Sometimes I think Mona is an angel come down from up there to answer everyone's questions.

"Why isn't he married?"

"Maybe he finally found her in the marketplace." That's Mona for you. She says things that stab you in the heart and she doesn't even know it. "Go to sleep," she says.

I look at the darkness around me. Shadows grow large and tall and then they engulf me. I close my eyes and think of small tiny kittens at the bottom of my bed.

Pineapples and the Sister

"He looks like a bird," Mona says, watching Enzo through thick glass. He swims toward us and waves at us behind the glass. With his cheeks full of air, his long hair wafting around him, he swims back and forth like a ruffled bird.

The only hotel in Zanzibar has a pool where you can swim to the bottom and watch people on the other side of the glass drinking coconut and pineapple drinks.

Pineapple is the perfect fruit; it's big and fancy and it's the only fruit to send to space for people out there who want to know what a fruit from our planet looks like.

"How about Porter's nephew?" Jack looks at me.

"What about him?" I ask.

"New boyfriend?" Jack's always suspicious of boys because he's jealous.

Mona and I say, "No way," at the same time and look at each other.

I can't stop thinking of Mo and that woman in the market. She has seen him naked and he has played with her hair. They're lying in bed and he brings her canned apricots in their sweet juice and he spoon-feeds her slowly. What am I going to do now?

Jack is in one of his "confession" moods. He doesn't usually talk about people much, but today, he wants to talk about Mo. I listen very carefully.

"I tried to get him girlfriends in London, but he never knew what to say to them," Jack begins. "He would take them to a film, drop them off and then go to his room and read magazines." Jack has a disgusting habit of cleaning his right ear with his small finger when he knows he is going to be talking for a while. "There was an Indian girl, though. I think she even made him take her upstairs to see his room." Jack shakes his head a little, looking at no one in particular. "I don't know why he hangs around here. Maybe he's just happy living the way he does with his mother."

"Let's ask Mo and Pina to come too," I hear Mother say.

I jump out of my thoughts and carefully ask, "Come where?" instead of asking who Pina is.

"Porter's party," Jack says, although he knows his first name.

Mona asks, "Who is Pina?" as she innocently puts a peanut in her mouth.

The moment before Mother answers seems like an eternity.

"A lot of people are going to be there," Jack says.

Mona and I wait for Mother's answer but somehow she doesn't hear us. I turn and look at Peter's and Enzo's legs beating in the water, and I desperately try to look indifferent. My mind is buzzing and I'm thinking so fast, I have a headache.

Finally I ask, "Who's Pina?"

Please, please, don't say it's his girlfriend.

"His sister from Canada," Mother says. I give out a low laugh and take a deep breath. I'm so happy I want to shout.

Mother starts going into detail about Pina's nice personality and beautiful hair and so on. I can't sit still; I want to walk around or do something. It's as if I have been chosen to accept a prize and I have to go up to the stage and get it.

"What happened to the Indian girl in London?" I ask.

"I don't know. Probably got married off." Jack gets up. "Now I have to go and *mayka the pee pee.*"

I want to go up and watch the curved white sails of the boats and smell the spices through the doorways and dark corners of Stone Town. Mona picks up her towel and before we go up the stairs, we hear Mother saying how concerned she is about us and what we're going to grow up to be. She wants us to grow up to be clean girls. I wonder how squeaky clean she wants us to be.

The Photo Album

We bought a photo album in Zanzibar and it has been haunting me since. Jack bought the photo album from a man with yellow teeth. The man came to our table when we were eating in one of those small café-like restaurants that smell of old raw meat and stale onions. There were flies everywhere, but Jack said we should eat where the natives eat. As soon as we sat down, the man with old tennis ball teeth opened up the photo album and started showing us the photos as if they were his mother's. He wore a black-and-white shirt with such small checkered patterns it made your eyes ache. We stopped eating and started looking at the photos. Maybe that's what people do with photos—stop everything and just stare at pictures—it's automatic. The man said, "Six dollars" to Jack, who was so amused he actually paid him and kept the album.

A woman's face stares into empty space. It's her photo album and she's in the photos, sometimes alone, sometimes with a man and sometimes there are just photos of African landscapes, or the ancient and narrow streets of

Zanzibar. The night pictures are creepy and cozy at the same time. The shops and restaurants that glow in the dark have curtains that are suspended in time forever. The vendors sit frozen and look back at you like noiseless observers. The pictures are just big enough to fit in the palm of my hand. Only one has a date written in long and beautiful handwriting that says July 6, 1965.

When we walk down the alleys in the real Zanzibar, the faces in the pictures look the same as in real life. I even think I recognize the vendors in the photos. The woman in the photo was pretty but her hair was so styled that you would think that she was not in Africa. She was blond and had a thin upper lip. Her eyes smiled at the photograph. In some photos, a small but strong dark man with searching eyes has his arms around her shoulders, like they have just become friends.

Now that I am holding pieces of paper with someone's images on it, I worry.

"She was pretty," I say. Peter holds the woman's picture in his hand and looks at it. He says, "Why was she with him?"

"Maybe she wasn't." Enzo is thinking.

"It's sad," I say.

One photo looks like a real holiday picture. The man has his arms around the woman's shoulders and they're standing in front of tiny huts. An African woman in the background leans against the door of her hut, holding a baby against her as if it has grown out of her waist. What does the black woman think about herself? Or the woman in front of her posing for the camera? Does she really live there?

Mona asks, "Why did she give her photos away?"

"The man probably stole it," Peter says, looking at a car in the photo. This reminds me of the time we were on a biology field trip, trying to figure out answers to everything we found on the ground.

"Maybe she just lost it," Mona says, turning the pages.

"I think she's dead," Enzo whispers into the quiet air.

I think, What if people who don't know me might someday sit somewhere and look at my pictures when I've become a ghost?

Tonight, before I fell asleep, my mind kept switching from the Indian woman in Mo's room in London to the woman in the photograph. What will I look like when I'm thirty-five? Will I have a man in a photograph with his arm on my shoulder? Where will Mo be? Where are those women now?

I will never own a photo album. Photographs are empty and scary and get left behind once you die. I don't ever want to die.

Lady

Mona has a photo of her cat, Lady, in the middle of the bright red book that she has been reading forever. She likes thick books, she says, because thin books can't be good. Lady came home one day limping and bloody and meowing so high, Mona said she was going to die. In the metal box at the animal doctor's room, Lady looked at us, scared. Mona had blood all over her blue school uniform. She cried, "I love you," again and again. "I love you. I love you." We left the office thinking why the doctor said he was going to put her to sleep instead of saying he's going to kill her with an injection. *Kill*, Mother said, is a violent word only evil people use.

Who are the evil people? Do evil people write down everything they hear around them? Or are they silent and talk only when people ask them questions? Evil people in films don't say much. They do things but they talk very little. My friend Ella can talk for hours and hours about nothing. I think if Mother stopped talking, then people might listen to her.

We're tucked under the fluffy clouds, on the tiny, shaking plane back to Dar es Salaam. Outside, I can see the bottom of the ocean. The greenish blue water is so clear, the coral reefs underneath wave back at me. The plane flies very low. Jack doesn't like to fly. He is sweating and not listening to anything Mother is saying. My guts are moving around in my head. I'm going to see Mo again.

Money and Amin

I'm getting used to Enzo now. As we lie by the pool, I think of Idi Amin and what he might have looked like when he was fourteen. Enzo says that he tortured people. "Just imagine," Enzo says, "this time last year, Idi Amin ordered his army to invade Tanzania but they were kept away with Nyererer's army." His hawkish eyes look through me and I think he knows about Mo.

Mo's woman in London must have been short and chubby and older than Mo. Her hair was cut short to her ears and every time she talked, she must have put her hand on his arm. Maybe she saw him in the Indian supermarket across from his flat where he shopped. She asked him if she could see his room. Putting yams and turmeric in his grocery basket, he must have told her that it was small and damp, but she said that she didn't care. She probably went upstairs and undressed; her round tummy, her full breasts and her dark pubic hair made him want to go and touch her. He went inside her warmness quick and then it was over. She must have got dressed and left and told him that she would call but she never did. He never saw her again. He must have wondered whether he should have done more but really didn't want to. He didn't like her smell.

That is how it was. I think.

Peter scuffs his feet when he walks. "Telephone," he says, turning back to the house. Could it be Mo? My eyes dart back and forth. I put my magazine away and get up too quickly. I'm dizzy. What will I say? Maybe he wants to meet me to go swimming and he will tell me about the woman in London.

"Who is it?" I ask Peter's back.

"Dad," he says. I start to run to the house because I know he's calling from New York and Jennifer doesn't want him to spend so much money.

Mona is on the telephone with him already. "Yes, OK, yes," and when she sees me she says, "OK. Bye. I'll give it to Tatum now." I take the phone and hear my father's unreal voice.

"How are you?" he asks. What if I tell him I'm in love, that I dream about a man at night who has dark hair, that I saw Mother naked before he left her and that I saw Jack go into that house with the wooden door and the smudged woman in the cubicle?

"Fine. How are you?" I say.

"Fine. How were your exams?"

"OK."

"OK means you'll get the best notes?"

I smile and he's not here to see me move my head to the right. Jack hasn't been home all day today. He left early in the morning and hasn't come back yet.

"How's New York?"

"Good."

"I wish you were here. It's so beautiful." *Beautiful, pretty, wonderful, great* and *fabulous* don't really say much if you don't see Africa. Adjectives are not enough to describe such places. That's why I look at clouds by myself because I can't explain them to anyone.

"I'm glad you like it. How's your mother?" She's my mother and not his wife, not someone he lay in bed with when she had her hair all open on the pillow, not when they kissed or he saw the darkness between her legs. She is my mother who hovers around me when I talk to him on the phone.

"She's fine. She says hi."

"Say hello to her."

Mother whispers in my ear, "Has he sent money?"

"I miss you," I say.

"I miss you, too. Did you get the money?" he asks.

"Mum says no. When can I see you?"

"I don't know, honey. Really, I don't know."

"OK."

"OK. So take care. I kiss you."

"Bye. I love you."

Mother doesn't wait a minute. "Same old cheap story. 'I've sent the money, honey.' He has enough for his whores." My forehead moves into wrinkles that I can't control when she says things like that. "Go get dressed," she says. "We're going to the Porters'."

She told me once that money is more important to her than her own life. I wish I could ask Idi Amin if he thought he was adopted when he was small and what is more important to him than his life.

Breasts and Mangos

I don't like parties. Parties are useless, but everyone wants to go to them. People sit on chairs or sofas, or they stand, talk and listen and drink too much. But God conversations are always the best at parties. I think of the woman who was with Mo at the marketplace. From behind, she looked like my aunt who went crazy. My aunt had long, dark shiny hair too. Everyone called her strange, but I knew she was too beautiful to be weird. Mother's crazy sister told me stories. She said that God changed beautiful people without personalities into blue butterflies. She said she knew a woman whose tongue had swollen so much she could hardly breathe. One day, the woman told her sister her secret and she could breathe again. Tonight, at the Porters' party, nobody is talking about God.

Mr. Porter's house is just like our house, only nicer. He has colorful Persian carpets on the floor and huge plants all around the house. This house looks lived in and ours looks rented. His living room is already glowing with people. There are four Americans, two Greeks, three Indian women, a Chinese man and two Germans. I come in and don't even have to think about anyone watching me. There are no real voices, just murmurs. "We never wanted children," a woman with straight, thick blond hair says. She wears a dark blue dress and looks like she is going to her office after the party.

A lumpy woman says, "After my children were born, my mother-in-law said, 'Always do what your husband tells you and you will be happy,' and I did and look at me now." Her face is a little swollen and she has a bald patch on top of her head. The more I look at her, the more swollen she looks—like a caterpillar standing.

Women talk about children who help out at home, and children who clean their rooms, and children who get good grades at school. I go through the greeting motions in my mind and think about the position of my head before I go into the room. Mother is in the next room telling other mothers whisperings of our lives, her tone rising and falling with each secret story. A woman says, "Isn't she an angel now?" and looks at me as if she has known me all her life. "Do you remember your grandmother? She died so young, the poor woman." Mother says it's fate that she has found Mrs. Moore, a childhood friend, here in Dar es Salaam.

Mrs. Moore looks a little like my grandmother. My grandmother was noiseless. We would walk around the house with her like flies around a bull and she would recognize us. Dad called her "senile" once but my grandmother knew who I was. She would lie on the bed like a queen with pillows around her. She was hypnotized by TV and Canada Dry.

Jack always looks harmless at parties, whether he talks about politics or cars, but when he drinks, he's not himself. When he gambles, he's not himself, either. He's like a child who wants to be a wolf. What does that woman in the old house with the cubicles think of Jack when he goes to her? Do they talk for hours by candlelight, or does he just lie on top of her?

Some of the guests eat as if they are alone in the room with no one watching them. Sitting on chairs, backs hunched or daydreaming, they bend their heads to the plates and bite into chicken legs and pull away the meat.

I think I see glimpses of Mo standing in a small crowd with his back to me. The silver-black hair is the same. I can even recognize his voice. It echoes in my head. If sounds like this were real, they would cut you through like little bits of glass. I turn my face to speak to Mr. Porter, who is standing with Enzo and some Greeks next to the buffet. Mo has seen me. I bet the Greek can hear my heart beat. I turn my face casually and catch Mo giving us a wave. Enzo and I go over to a woman and Mo, and I wipe my sweaty hands on my dress.

He says, "Is your chick becoming a young hen?"

"It's growing," I say.

He turns to the woman with long shiny black hair and perfect white teeth, "This is Pina, my sister. This is Tatum, and you're Enzo." His hand gesture is so small, I could hardly see it. The woman is the one with perfect calves who was holding Mo's arm at the marketplace.

She says hello with a voice that sounds like a harp. She asks us all sorts of questions. How long we're staying, if we like it here, what we've done till now. She is pretty with her shiny hair and light brown skin.

"Mo was never ambitious," Pina says, looking at him lovingly. "He could have been a pilot but he just didn't want to do the math and physics in school." I can look all the way down her blouse if I get closer. She has hard, well-formed breasts under the blouse. Enzo stares at her. "He was good at poetry and reading," Pina continues. "I bet he could be a writer if he wanted." Mo is not really paying attention. He looks over at the Greek man who is surrounded by three women. Are men full of charm because they learned it from TV or a hero they've read about while growing up?

Pina acts like Mo's big sister. He looked so young standing next to her. I can't smile at him; I can't do anything. I only answer back politely and look around and try to catch his eye as I turn my head. I want to memorize all the details of his face, so that when I go to bed at night I have a better picture of him.

There's a drunken man telling an Indian man about some mangos he's exporting to Miami and how he has to fly there tomorrow. The German talks of his tennis game from yesterday; he speaks English as if he is forcing words out of his throat with difficulty. The shiny Indian woman looks around quietly.

One woman has stepped fresh out of the hairdresser's. Her unnaturally gigantic curls stand perfect and there is a bubble of hair spray smell around her colorful face. She has a squeaky laugh and it comes and goes every ten minutes. Sometimes I think women like this are all from one mold. All with the same hairstyle, the same way they eat and laugh, all from the same master. They look so womanly but in the wrong way. There's another man sitting on the sofa with cartoon eyes. He smiles at everyone as he looks through you. His buttery eyes are not quite there. His glass is tipped so low he might spill the drink any minute. A short woman wearing a light green pantsuit smokes a long thin cigar and puffs smoke at a big man's face. She has a wicked smile as if she is up to something.

Then there is another man who looks like Father Christmas. His hair is white and he wears kind glasses and talks as if he would like to give presents. I wander around and watch. They're playing Barry Manilow songs. I know I'm not supposed to like these kinds of gooey songs, but it seems OK right now. I sit on the sofa next to Mona and Enzo. Enzo gets up and stretches his thin hand to me. I don't really want to dance, but I get up anyway. The minutes go on like hours. I want to go to my room and read or lie on my bed and think about Mo. I want to talk to Mona. When the music stops, I go looking for her. On the balcony there are two shadows. One of them belongs to Mo. His voice says, "I like my job. It's easy enough, sometimes it gets hot, but people leave me alone and I don't have a boss to tell me what to do." Pina and Mo have their backs to me. "I just get the stuff in the morning, sign off for it and organize the warehouse."

"This is not a life—a grown man living with his mother."

"I have a good routine. I'm happy; I don't want things to change." I turn to go back in. Then Pina says, "Do you think that girl has a crush on you?" I don't like the way she says "that girl". I step back a little.

"Who?"

"Tatum." Pina says my name as if she has known me for years.

"Tatum? How can she? She's just a little girl."

"I'm telling you. She is infatuated with you. Girls her age get crushes like that over older men. I know."

"She's just a child. There isn't anything even womanly about her."

"There wasn't a single time when I didn't have crushes on my teachers. . . ." I try to hear the rest but the rush of blood to my head is stopping me from listening. The crickets chirp and the dogs bark angrily, but I can't hear Mo's and Pina's voices anymore. I hold my hand over my mouth to stop myself from breathing.

BACK IN THE LIVING ROOM, my heavy feet take me upstairs to one of the bathrooms. I lock the door and stare at my own reflection in the mirror. I don't recognize myself; it's someone else. My eyes could be anybody's. I close my eyes and when I open them, something has happened to me here. I can't tell what it is, but I know it's something terrible. My eyes dart from one side to the other, like when you try to catch the images from a moving train. I can't think. Colors and the lines of the tiles on the bathroom floor fade with every thought. It's as if a thousand thoughts are going through my head but it's still empty. The thoughts just rush past me and I'm too slow to stop them and make out their shape. I look at the deep loneliness of the bathroom tiles and see myself for the first time.

A knock on the door brings my thoughts back down to the mirror and the bathroom colors. I open the door and Father Christmas smiles at me. He locks the door and I can hear him moving in the bathroom. Finally, I come down the stairs trying not to show any expression. Mona looks at me once and then turns again a second time and stares at me. I hear Enzo telling her, "I like Mo. He's cool."

I can feel my teeth grinding and it hurts. My tongue just moves around my mouth without a direction. The rest is just a blur of words—"My daughter is at the . . . the color doesn't match well . . . humid and hot. There isn't enough paper . . . do you know what I mean?"

Then there is no noise, like when you wake up in the morning and think that everyone in the house is still asleep. You look up at the ceiling and remember little slices of your dream. Some time later, you get up and go downstairs to the garden and see everyone sitting around the breakfast table. And all this time you thought you were the only one awake.

I leave the party and go back to our house in the dark; I don't look at a single mirror on the way out. The moon looks so small and bitter I wonder who thought of putting an ugly, white dusty thing up in the sky. The quiet darkness in our house reminds me of Christmas Eve, when you wait all night for the day to come.

I sit by the phone in the hall and stare at the newspaper on the table. I dial his number.

"Hello? Dad?"

"Tatum. Why are you calling?" his voice sounds so near I want to cry.

"I just wanted to call." I look at the picture of corpses covered with colorful cloths in the magazine.

"Is everything OK? Do you have money?"

"Yes. Do you think of us?" There's a haze in front of my eyes and I can't even look at the beautiful beige shoes one of the women is wearing. In the picture she is bending down to look for bodies under the rubble.

"Listen, this is a bad time to call. I'll call you back on the weekend, how's that?"

"Bye." I stare at the newspaper. Earthquake in Turkey. The woman's face in the newspaper is so white and gentle. People do everything wrong here. They don't know how to act, what to say, how to stand, how to eat, how to listen. In my room, I can be invisible. I can look out the window and make a row out of my books. No one can see what I do.

It starts to rain, but the rain isn't just rain in Africa—it's the monsoon. A strong fragrance rises off the ground.

The flood of rain is heavy and loud and I think of the dry, greedy grass outside. It just sits there with its roots below, and doesn't think of names people call it. If I were grass, then I could empty myself of everything. I would feel the earth inside me and pretend that my blades are empty.

"What's up?" Peter suddenly has appeared. I can tell from the tone of his voice that he is not in his teasing mood.

"Did Jack send you?"

"No, are you a zombie?" He picks up a book and flips the pages like he's looking for something in the middle. "What's up?" he asks.

"*Nichts*," I say in German. If we were allowed to speak only ten sentences every day, what would we choose to say? Would I tease? Would I joke with Peter?

Peter says, "One thing I wanted to tell you—you should like what makes you different."

"What?"

"Hey, I think you're cool." It sounds as if another voice is talking from inside of him. I wonder if that's what happens when people say they're hearing voices. Maybe it's really their own voice coming from somewhere else.

I don't know that what Peter says has to do with anything but I say, "Right," and put on a Donna Summer cassette in the tape player. Peter puts the book down and says, "You know, I brought you and your chicken some mangos." He hands me the neatly cut mangos on a plate and turns and closes the door behind him. I look at the orange and yellow mangos that I know will taste sour and sweet and tangy, just like I know that Peter is my brother.

Baked Beans

Do girls wake up one day and say, "From today I'm going to be a housewife"? Not a dentist or a stewardess or a ballet dancer? They look after their babies and feed them, make the beds while the sun shines in through the bedroom. There would never be anybody home, just the woman and the sound of her work or maybe the radio or the TV. Loneliness might be a housewife.

If Mother was Indian, we might live in a room above a store in Dar es Salaam. She might cook rice and curry, with the swift hand of a woman who has cooked all her life. Her hair would be long and shiny and black with strands of white hair in between. Her friends might come by with samosas and sweet Indian dishes.

Now when I think back, Mother has never had friends. There were people she knew, but never friends. When did she stop having friends? When did she stop saying to her girlfriend that she would get sweaty hands when she saw the boy she daydreamed about?

Once, when Mother said to me, "You know, I sometimes think that Mona is my mother," I thought she was joking. I looked away from her hunched shoulders, and I looked at the veins on my wrist, thinking I have such nice violet and blue veins. Mother tells Mona everything and I find out years later. Just like the time when Mother married Jack, Mona knew before I did. Imagine not knowing that your own mother has gotten married. Imagine that.

When I marry, I won't tell *her*.

I can't stop thinking about what Mo said to his sister about me. I don't ever want to look into his face again. I'm angry at Mother for making me go to the supermarket with her. She wants to know if there is a conference in Dar es Salaam to which I have to go, because I'm in such a hurry. I walk fast because our steps echo as we walk into the cool supermarket that looks almost empty. We are the only people in the warehouse-like building. There are one or two of each item on the shelves but some shelves are completely empty. Mother looks at labels to read all the ingredients before she puts them in the basket. She puts on her reading glasses for each can and reads the grams and compares them to another one. Shillings don't have any value, anyway, and I've given up trying to figure out how much something is in pounds. I don't see why she just can't buy what she wants and get out of here.

"I don't know how these people can afford the prices," Mother says.

"They can't; that's why it's empty," says Mona.

"Choose one," I say to Mona, holding out Colgate and Dentagard.

"Baked beans," Mother says, taking down her glasses. "I miss them. Ask them if they have any."

In the Swahili phrase book there is no baked beans. I walk around the empty aisles and think if the canned goods pay the rent here. The woman at the cash desk has her hair in rainbow-beaded braids that shine like olive oil. She looks up from her magazine with the Three Degrees on the cover and says, "No, we don't have baked beans."

"That sounds nice," Mother says, meaning the braided woman's accent. She looks like a woman who has friends. Her black shiny skin looks ripe and fresh, almost holy. If she were an angel, she would be the angel of light. Does the angel in braids leave notes on the fridge door for her children, just like Mother did, that read, "Eat potatoes and beans in oven." And would she leave another note in her daughter's bedroom, "Eat potatoes and beans in oven," just in case the daughter doesn't see the first one?

"Ask her where I can buy whole-wheat bread," Mother whispers so the woman doesn't hear.

"She speaks English, Mother," Mona murmurs.

A real mother would know how to act. I won't act like her when I'm that old. I won't repeat things like she does. If only she could save her sentences and say them when she needs them. "How do you cook pasta sauce again?" she would ask me whenever I came in the kitchen in London. A real mother would remember how to cook. I don't want to teach her things. "How about marmalade?" she asks Mona to ask the woman. A real mother would have her own voice. I'm embarrassed.

Mona goes to the other side of the aisle and looks at the plastic flowers. She looks at the strangest things as if she would buy them any minute to put on some imaginary mantelpiece.

"Do you think they have Coffeemate?" Mother asks again.

I think of Mo and of Pina's perfect calves. "Girls her age." How does she know my age? Father Christmas's face appears in my head and I don't want to believe in anything anymore. "Just shut up," I whisper and then regret it the minute it leaves my mouth. Mother stares at me, pressing her lips together. There is something scary in her eyes. She turns to Mona and says, "She's gone too far."

Mona gives me a look of disbelief.

"I do everything for you and this is the way you treat me." She will now tell me how she gave up her life for us; she could have been somebody, done something if it weren't for us. And she will end her speech by saying that I'm ungrateful. I can't tell her that it's her fault that she doesn't like her life. That it's her fault for sticking around with us for so long. It's her fault for marrying the wrong men. I wish she would grow up and be my mother.

Mother goes to one of the back aisles so she won't have to look at me.

I explain to Mona, "People were staring."

"There wasn't anyone there," Mona says.

"She doesn't do anything right," I say.

"That's the point," Mona says. "We are not all perfect." I wonder where she learned to talk like this.

"I didn't say that."

"Why should you care what other people think of us?" Already I think of an answer for her, but she says, "Or what Dad thinks of you?" I look at a can on the shelf in front of me, and I swear they're baked beans. I want to cry.

"What are you talking about?" I wish I could hear Mo's voice.

"The attention and everything," Mona says. She knows that I used to put bandage strips on my fingers in the morning before school so that people would ask me what happened.

"What's that supposed to mean?"

She looks across at the canned food on the shelves, picks up a can and walks back toward the cashier. Then she asks, "Don't you wonder why he never calls? We always have to call him."

"He calls on my birthdays."

"Don't be so naive. Mum calls him." I know Mona isn't lying. "Then she pretends that he's the one who called."

I look at Mother's face but she just walks away to the cash desk. She looked like that when I saw her sitting alone in the balcony in London. The smell of fresh grass came from downstairs and I held my breath to keep it in as long as I could. She sat there with a bowl of soup and spooned the liquid in through her lips. Face down and shoulders hunched, she didn't see me. She just sat there like a little girl in a corner, drinking her soup. Her face was sad and I wanted to go and hold her and tell her that she's OK. I went to my room and I could hear the spoon hitting the side of the bowl. I wonder when it happened? When did Mother find out that she was old or that she didn't have any friends? I think that was the first time I felt sorry for her. Mona puts the can on the table in front of the cash desk; Mother looks at the baked beans and smiles. I will not talk today.

When I think of Jack, I think of poker, stained shirts and warm whisky breath. He loses in poker, in blackjack and every other game that I can think of. He sits at the round table in the house with his white tank top and his belly bulging out above his tight shorts, looking like a professional poker player. He fits well in Africa; he's scrubby and bushy and he smells of heat.

Mr. Porter sits at Jack's right side and a greasy-haired American with impractical white skin is to Jack's left. His first name is his last name; I think his name is Mr. George. Peter lies on the couch watching a man in a business suit giving an interview on TV, talking about those "uninformed environmentalists." Mo sits at the poker table with his back to the door. I can only see the back of his head when we enter the living room.

Mother must have made a face at Jack when coming in because as soon as he sees me he says, "Go upstairs, love; I'll be up in a minute." I look out the window and wish Mo would look at me. I walk into the kitchen and open the fridge door and look for something to drink. Peter sits up and takes a quick look at Jack.

"Go upstairs, Tatum," he says louder. I wish I had his voice, then everyone would be scared of me.

Mo and the other men look down at their cards, either embarrassed or amused. I am so mad I could scream. My head is a jumble of words. And Mo is here.

"You can't tell me what to do," I say, looking straight at Jack, "you illiterate, old slob." I'm frightened of the silence and the shuffling of the feet under the poker table.

Jack says calmly, "Go up now." The lump in my throat stops me from crying. Mo is going to think that I'm like those spoiled brats you see on TV, but brats are only brats if they don't know it.

On the way up, I hear Jack's muffled voice saying, "She thinks she's royalty." Mother says something and Jack says, "Illiterate, old slob—very good."

Mother will probably say that I'm getting worse and Mr. Porter will say that it's part of growing up and that he used to be like that. Mother will say that Mona was never like that.

My room smells of Ras's droppings. I have to keep him outside from now on. On my bed, I chew on my split nails to make them even. My fingers smell of Mother.

There isn't anything womanly about Pina; I think I hate her.

In London, there is a card in my room with the picture of the planet Earth. There's the perfect outline of Africa with its brown-creamy color. The map of Africa looks like a screaming woman, but sometimes it's a woman who's just yawning. The Earth looks like a perfectly round magic crystal with white strands of clouds and blue oceans. This is the one picture I want in my head when I die.

There's a knock on the door and Mo's voice says, "Are you OK?" I want him to come in. I want to tell him that I feel like crying and that I hate everyone. My voice sounds nervous. "Yes, thank you." I get up and stand behind the closed door so he doesn't see me smile. He wouldn't have come up if he didn't care. I could ask him why he called me a little girl. I could ask him why he doesn't see me as a woman. I could ask him if he loves me. So he *does* like me. Why didn't anybody else come up, Mona or Peter or Jack? Maybe he's too shy to tell me he likes me. He came up because he cares.

"I came up to say bye, and if you need anything, let me know," he says.

I hold on to my breath as long as I can, then give out a heavy gulp of air.

"Thanks."

I put on my sandals, change into a white dress and rush downstairs. Mother and Jack are at the table drinking tea. It's as if Mo never came upstairs or was never here. His car isn't outside, either. I go out through the kitchen to the ocean.

The sun is meant to be up there. There is no other place it could be. On the water, it wouldn't float. It has to be on top of the ocean, making it shine. And there is no red in the ocean. Even here, sitting on the sand, there is no red as far as my eyes can see.

"Coconuts, miss?" the man's voice startles me. He stands above me with a basket of coconuts on his shoulders. His black, shiny eggplant skin smells of old dust.

"No, *asante*," I say.

He moves like a shadow. He stares at me and smiles with white teeth that stand in a perfect row.

"Very good coconuts." His red T-shirt has holes in it and his pants are torn. The small straw hat on his head makes him look silly. I want him to leave.

He narrows his eyes and I think he's going to sneeze. Then he says, "You look like my dead brother." I tremble and suddenly want to be in the house eating vanilla pudding with Mona. The man's lean silhouette is raw and he has carved cheekbones. His blue-black lashes don't move when he talks.

"When I think of my brother, I want to sing old songs, miss." Then he starts humming a song that I know I've heard before. His red eyes are glazed.

All around me the folds and curves of the sand have disappeared. Palm trees tower over me and I know that if I die now, I will never know if Mona would sing songs for me. Would she just keep some things of mine? How would she decide what to keep and what to throw away when I die?

The man's red eyes are too open. I can see everything. I can smell his wishes of wanting to touch me. His mouth, opened just a little, and the tongue I can imagine moving in his mouth. I don't want him to touch me.

Mother's voice comes nearer and I take in a deep breath. The eggplant man just stands there and hums. Then he packs his basket and goes the same way he came.

"Don't get anything from them," Mother's voice says before I can even see her. "You never know what diseases you'll get." Coming toward me, Mother's fast steps and Jack's slow walk make them look out of step. They reach me at the same time.

I turn and look at the red color getting smaller until it becomes a fading red dot on the sand. If I look at the man's figure long enough, and then look at the ocean, I can see the red.

Dad's Friend

Pina is going back to Toronto. We go through the departure ceremony, the kisses and hugs. If she wasn't Mo's sister, she might have been my friend. She might have told me I'm too young. It's so hard to keep a secret. I want to tell her that he came upstairs and asked me how I was, or that I think about him at night. I can't tell anyone. When they drive away, I imagine her telling Mo to be careful of me. I don't think I would want her as a friend, anyway.

In my bedroom, I write in my diary that Pina has left. I want to write something else but I don't know what. I don't want to write a poem because poems are for dreamy people. Poets are weak and they're short and sweaty and wear thick glasses. I'm not a poet.

Dad's friend in Greece was sweaty, too. His breathing was heavy but he had a kind face. He was there on my tenth birthday and he touched me. That was the first time I had my birthday on our school holiday. Mona and I would climb all over Dad's friend because he was short and round and he was the kindest man I knew. Mona was lying on the sand and Peter was swimming. Dad's friend suddenly picked me up from behind and threw me in the water. Then he said, "Come on, I'll throw you again." He told me to turn my back to him and raise my hands. Then, slowly, he picked me up from under my armpits and put his hands over my small breasts. I thought he had large hands and it must have been an accident. When he kept his hands there and rubbed my breast, I knew he liked it. We swam farther away from Peter until I couldn't feel the sand underneath my feet. "Come on, I'll throw you again," he said and pulled me toward him and turned me around, touching my breasts again. I knew he liked it, so I let him. It was so strange; I didn't have to do anything. I just raised my arms and he felt me. I knew this was something I should never tell Mother.

I showed photos of Greece to Auntie Gloria back in London. She saw the one with Dad's friend and Mona and me with his arm over our shoulders. She looked up at Mother and said, "You shouldn't leave them alone with this man." Then she asked me who he was and I thought and I thought, but I couldn't remember his name.

I still can't remember Dad's friend's name.

Scorpions

There's a mist in front of my eyes that doesn't fade away. If Mo called me darling, it might dissolve. There's a jumble of feelings in my head that don't make sense. Everything is split up into little pieces, and I don't know how to put them in order. You can't put secrets in order, either. It's like the plane you sit in that is flying through the air. It's all so normal but it's a secret, too. How can it fly?

Peter, Mona and I watch the boat cutting the silver-gray and green water as Mo drives the boat to a little island that he says is a tourist attraction because nobody lives there. There's a calm silence around the warm bubble inside the boat.

"What does Pina do in Toronto?" Peter asks.

"She teaches," Mo says.

Enzo didn't come; he went on safari with Salim.

I'm glad Mo is here and not Dad. When I think of Dad, I think of spaces in between, and even Jack reminds me of large dark holes, but Mother is never-ending. Jack is happy to sleep all day and get up in the afternoon, shower, comb his hair, put on his aftershave and go to play poker. Mother finds things to do in the house; she doesn't lounge around much; she's just like Mona. They don't take naps or lie down like I do. Mona and Mother have to move, as if one day, if they stop moving, they will die.

Mo turns off the engine and we sit there listening to the water hitting the side of the boat. The yellow and orange colors cover the mountain in the distance like a heavy blanket. The sound of crickets gets louder as the half moon comes out from behind a cloud.

"See the fish?" Mo points to the water.

Everything is quiet. It's the silent noise that I will remember the most. Getting stranded on a desert island is my favorite daydream. In the dream, I wake up on the sand, tired and my clothes torn. Mo comes to me, caresses my hair and carries me in his arms. He makes us a hut on top of a tree and I cook for him. We take walks on the sand and hold each other at night. We have to stay there for years before we're rescued. We might even have children.

If everyone thought up the same dreams and they didn't know it, would they be dreams still?

We get to the island with a muffled thump and get out of the boat. Mona and Peter jump out by themselves, but Mo holds his hand out to me. He is going to notice that my hand is sweaty. I think he looks at my face when he holds my hand, but I'm not sure. The blond sand is full of algae and dead, yellow palm leaves. The strong hot breeze feels like a giant hairdryer blowing in your face. Mo walks confidently, his head turned down slightly, and his arms hang down long and strong. We walk into the wooded area and Mo points to the different vegetation.

The colors and the shapes of the leaves are too green and too big. Everything about them is exaggerated, as if someone took the trouble of making them by hand to go with the gigantic, perfect trees. Some leaves have stems of elaborate flowers that are orange, red and yellow all in one. They look sculptured. They will never wilt or die. They will live forever.

Birds call from all directions, maybe talking about us. Their calls have a rhythm. Some only call twice, and some call continuously and then finally stop. The ones who chatter take over the ones who're quiet. Mother once said that when she was small, she thought she could talk to animals. She would listen to them for hours and pretend in her mind that she was talking.

We sit down at a clearing and listen to the sounds around us. Maybe if I were a little nastier and stronger, then Mo would like me. He might think I'm more interesting if I wasn't nice. I could be like those girls Mother warns me about. Like Drew, who Mother says is a bad influence. The world could be made up of mothers warning their daughters about other mothers' daughters. Somebody could be warning her child about me right now, and somebody else might warn her daughter about that child. It feels good to think somebody is being warned about me.

When I know Mo's not looking, I stare at his lips, his eyes, his hands and his neck. I want to remember all the details for my desert island dream. I wish I had a picture of him. The only picture I have is the one Peter took of us, but it's faded. Our faces are so faint, Mo could be anybody. Somebody might think that I'm in love with just anybody.

Mona and I sit on a tree stump and look up at the tall moving trees. It makes me feel dizzy. My legs are stretched out with my hands behind my torso. My legs look thinner stretched out, and now that they are brown, they look even better. The humid air has made my hair curly and bouncy. I run my hands through my hair and pretend to watch the clouds. Mo looks at my legs and then looks away. For the first time, I feel pretty.

If I had one wish, I would wish that Mo would fall in love with me. I get up and walk around the clearing. There's a little footpath leading to another clearing. I look quiet and mysterious just like *Cosmopolitan* told me. It told me about "how to find your dream man and keep him." It said that you should never give away too much about yourself, "be a challenge to your man so that he has to find some secrets about you." But I'm not like that. I want to tell everyone my secrets, and I want them to tell me what they think. How can I keep things to my-self? I want to tell Mo everything. But *Cosmopolitan* must be right because it has these beautiful women inside the magazine who know how to keep a man. I have to get Mo. I don't know what to be anymore—the tempting, secretive girl or just myself.

Drew had told me to act feminine that day when we went to the cinema in London with Glenn and Wayne. They were fooling around with cigarettes and showing off that they could catch the glowing cigarette butt. I had said, "Anyone can do that," and Glenn tossed the glowing cigarette butt at me. I caught it in my hand and we all laughed. Then Drew told me that I was stupid and that boys don't like girls who do guy things and that I should pretend that I'm gentle and sweet so guys like me. Drew always put on her high, sweet voice when boys were around. I couldn't recognize her.

I wish there was another me, a double of me somewhere that I don't know about. Mona hands out the sandwiches and fruits that Mother has packed for us. Afterward, we pack our stuff and start walking back to the boat. I walk a little slower and look around dreamily. Mo turns his head and slows down. He says, "Is something wrong?"

"No." He thinks I'm sulking.

"One minute you're friendly," he says with a smile, "and the next minute you're quiet," he says.

I don't want to be too mysterious. "It's nothing," I say.

"Are you homesick? Do you miss your friends?" he asks.

"I don't know," I say. This is a good answer, I think.

In my head, I imagine him asking me what's wrong and I tell him that I don't want to go back to London and that I feel lonely, and he says I should come and live with him and that he will look after me and take care of me and love me.

I push aside the palm leaves with my foot as I walk. Then I see them—two black scorpions dancing. They don't seem to pay any attention to us. They hold each other's claws and they dance a quick tango. I stand over them and watch.

"Don't move." Peter had told me that scorpions can't stay in the sun more than twenty minutes or they will die. "How would you like to be a scorpion? Racing for your life when the sun comes up?" he had asked me.

"Give me your hand." I could drown in Mo's voice. "Walk back two steps with me slowly." He really holds my hand. I walk back two steps, feel his hand, the skin and the warmth of his hand. If only Mona and Peter weren't here. Mo still holds my hand as we walk slowly away from the dancing scorpions. When we step on the boat, he lets go of my hand. He looks tired and white in the face.

On the boat, I feel heavy and drunk when the sun sets. Yellow and orange covers the mountain far away, and the sound of the crickets gets louder as the moon shines over us. The moon has shadows all over it. There's a mist that just hangs there. When the sun goes down, leaves shine from both sides. They're sunny underneath and dark on top. There's a sudden burst of brightness before the sun goes, and if I didn't know it, and had woken up right at that moment, I might have thought it was sunrise.

Before it went dark, there was one moment when the buzzing of flies and the constant hissing of the crickets stopped. It was like the silence right before a conductor lifts his baton to conduct an orchestra—one second of stillness and then, noise. Mo held my hand all the way to the boat.

Mother

"We're accumulating," Mother's neighbor, Mrs. Birken, said to her one day. It made Mother flinch without even noticing it herself. Afterward, I went upstairs to check the word in the dictionary to make sure that I had understood Mrs. Birken. It wasn't that I didn't understand; it was just that when Mother had asked her how she was doing, "accumulating" didn't seem the right answer from Mrs. Birken, who always smelled of anchovies.

Mother was named after her dead sister, at least that's what she told me. Soon after she was born, her eight-year-old sister died in a fire. My grandmother couldn't think of a new name for Mother, so she named her after her dead sister. Mona told me that Mother had a bad childhood and that's why she has this thing with money and doesn't look people straight in the face.

I watch her when Mother thinks I'm not looking. Sometimes, she looks like she is lost in a maze and can never get out. Sometimes, she looks as if she is in pain and might just burst out crying. Mother was always ashamed of my grandmother. "Imagine that," she told Mona and me in the kitchen once. Mother put down the vegetable peeler, turned to us and said, "Imagine being ashamed of your own mother." But when Mother screams, "Do you know how much that's costing me?" when I'm on the phone with my friends, I am ashamed of her, too. The word *money* is in everything, she says. She goes out and comes back saying how much she spent and what things cost. She came back one day, showed me a grocery slip where she had circled the amount on it. "That man, he screwed me." Then she disappeared and drove all the way to the store to get the few pennies back. It's funny, really, but Jack says it's sick. Mother says that when she was a child, her family was poor; nevertheless, her mother would spend everything they had on stupid things. She had vowed that she would never spend like my grandmother. Did she ever think what it would be like if her mother had died? And when she did die, was it Mother who had wished her dead?

I saw two mothers in Hyde Park one day. One of them was sitting by her child playing on the grass. The other was standing on the pathway holding a pram. Her child was just wandering around by itself. I remember thinking that the woman on the pathway was my mother; she would never get herself dirty on the grass for me.

I asked Mona whether she knew that Mother was named after her dead sister, and she said, "It's not true. Mother just made that up."

Peter didn't come shopping with us today. I don't know how he ever gets the things he has because he doesn't shop. Mother occasionally buys him something, but he never goes shopping. If this were a story, I would make up something like fairies bringing his clothes and toys to his bed at night. Maybe Peter has a magic closet that he enters and goes into another world filled with shops.

Mother says I'm the only girl she knows who doesn't like shopping for clothes. I know that girls go shopping together, and I know that it is fun to try on clothes. I know that they laugh and giggle; I've seen it on TV. When I go out with girlfriends, I'm supposed to go to changing rooms, take my clothes off, put on new clothes and match them with something. I should giggle, but it isn't that funny—it's just silly. But I go with them anyway because some things you're supposed to do when you're a girl. You are supposed to blush and look annoyed when boys swear in front of you, just to make them see you don't like it. But how am I supposed to know all this? Who told me I shouldn't ask a boy out and I shouldn't call? No one told me to give their presents back when it's over. I didn't know I shouldn't let them touch my breasts on the first date. I don't think I would change if I let a boy touch my breasts. Mother never told me any of this.

Mona and I have to buy gold for the party tonight.

Here in Dar es Salaam, shops are either half empty or packed full of products. The shop underneath Mo's room is packed to the ceiling with mattresses. The supermarket is half empty. The jewelry shops are filled with gold. Gold is a good investment, Mother has been telling us as far back as I can remember. Her jewelry box is so full that every time she opens it, chains and rings and bracelets fall out. I don't think she's ever going to sell it, and nobody would buy it from her anyway.

The gold shops we go to have iron bars in front of the windows and doors. The doors are locked, and after knocking a few times, the owner or the security man opens it for you.

125

A short Indian woman opens the shop door after she checks that we look OK. We enter a room like Aladdin's cave. There is so much gold here that I don't know if we are ever going to choose something and get out. The strange thing is that it doesn't smell of anything. If you close your eyes here, in this shop full of gold, you couldn't tell what the small Indian woman is selling.

"I want a set. A very simple set," Mother tells the woman without looking at her, "nothing too ornamental."

The uniformed man watches us through the window from outside. If I stared at people the way he does, I would be embarrassed. I think maybe people who stare at you have something to tell you but they can't. I let my eyes glide from the security man to the shiny necklaces, bracelets and rings.

"This one?" From the jungle of gold Mona has chosen something. She's picky and so she always finds the perfect things. She's the one who orders the best food, which I end up wanting. She buys the nicest clothes that I want. She tries on a necklace and it's perfect.

"It's too small," I say.

"I don't want anything bigger," she says. She takes it off and puts it on the counter and walks around looking inside the glass cases.

There are two pictures hanging above her. There's a sea animal on one of them, "*Walrus/Kibokobarafu.*" It looks like a huge seal with long sharp white teeth. In the background, there is snow and ice and the seal is sitting on a frozen riverbed. The word *Tanzania* is written beneath it in black ink, but neither the animal nor the scenery is from here. In the other picture, there's an African hunter with a bow and arrow. It looks like a painting by a twelve-year-old. The hunter carries a bow and arrow and wears a yellow tank top and beige shorts. He looks like a tourist aiming at a herd of realistic-looking antelopes grazing on the grass. On top of the painting it says "Traditional Hunter." I don't know who painted those, but they can't be from Tanzania.

The sales lady shakes her head and says, "That's my last price." When I'm old, I will not act like Mother and say mean things and think back to the bad childhood that I've had. Mother is proud of her victory today. Saving shillings and pence makes her feel good. Maybe that's what has made her face look like it does.

"What are you going to wear?" Mona asks me.

"I'm going to buy a new dress," I tell her. Mother gives out one of her huh's and grins. She looks like a monster. "You're crazy," she says. "Here in Dar es Salaam?" When she says I'm crazy, she really means it. She doesn't say it as a joke. I am her crazy daughter and she won't see me any other way. I'm her lazy daughter who can never make up her mind. I don't know what kind of a person I'm going to grow up to be. But she's the one who raised me, so she must have done something wrong.

The Indian woman gives us directions to the home of a woman who sells "beautiful European dresses." We cross the street and see two American men who look like priests, and do not belong in the scenery, go toward the jewelry store.

There are women sitting in little rooms by the street sewing colorful dresses. The heat does not seem to bother them. The dresses have animal patterns on them—giraffes or a whole elephant face taking up the space on the dress. There are no small patterns, only large ones. The women look up from their sewing and look right through me. Their look is hazy and frozen in time; they are somewhere else, anywhere but here in the heat.

127

We pass a man who is sitting on the floor repairing shoes with his bare hands. His hands are so fast we stop to watch him. He picks up a shoe, and with quick hand movements, he puts a piece of material on the shoe to fix a hole. Then he picks up the other shoe and does the same thing in seconds, one movement dissolving into the other. No one is there waiting for the shoes to be fixed, but he does it so quickly, as if he's in a hurry. A small hill of shoes lies next to him, and I want to see what he's going to do when he is done with the heap, or where the customers are and when they will come and what he will do. But no one comes.

The building where the dresses are supposed to be is old. We go up the dark, musty-smelling stairs and Mother knocks on the wooden door. As if by magic, the door opens and the whiff of sweet Indian perfume and women's voices smother me. The cool air in the room makes the colorful saris and dresses hanging around the walls seem alive. There are so many women here, I want to look at every one of them, their different faces. I want to lie here and listen to their voices, to inhale their perfume. Big women, slim women, pretty faces and chubby faces with moles on their cheeks or red dots on their foreheads. Their long straight black hair, so shiny, reflecting the purple tinge of their saris. Their chatter is something that I've gotten used to, a mixture of Hindi and English.

A big woman with a beautiful shiny face and bright red lipstick floats toward us. Her walk is majestic.

"Hello, my dears. Mrs. King is my name." I think maybe she knows Mother. "What can I offer you today?"

Mother looks at the room with clothes hanging everywhere and says without wasting time, "There's a party tonight."

"Ah, the Zebra Club party. Look around. I will help you find a dress," and with a wink she says, "I'll give you a good price." She follows us around her rooms like a cat.

Her squeaky, high voice reminds me of Aunt. Dad's sister had a shrill voice that never lost its strength. My fat aunt would hug and kiss me. Holding my hand, she would say things like "You were gorgeous when you were a little girl. You remember how everyone loved you? You were the most beautiful child in the family." Then she would lick her lips and say, "She's still beautiful," as if I wasn't in the room, "but she was more beautiful then. Now she's got her father's nose and her mother's chin." Stroking my hair, she would tell Mother that maybe I should get a haircut. I think that when I'm older, I will tell her how fat she is while she strokes my hair and holds my hand and says, "You've got such lovely wavy hair. You should let it grow longer. Men like long hair." The last time I saw Aunt, she looked old. Her hair had strands of gray and her skin around her cheeks and under her neck was sagging. She had that inflated look about her. Her lips fluttered every time she talked and the girlish tone was just like Mrs. King's.

The dresses in Mrs. King's overlighted room are too puffy and ornamental to even try on. I can't wear any of them to the party because they're from ten years ago. There's one simple black dress that might fit me. It's a little short and small but that's all there is.

"Beautiful, spectacular," Mrs. King says, as if she's in the theater.

"It's too tight and too short," Mother says.

Mona says, "Wow."

Mrs. King says, "It's time to marry your daughters, no?"

I have thought of this so often. I imagine myself in a white wedding gown walking next to a man who puts a ring on my finger. When a woman told my Mother about her "other half," Mona and I giggled because we imagined half the woman going to work, and the other half of her body staying at home and looking after her kids. A ring and a man, forever, seem like a bad joke. When I dream of Mo, I don't see myself married like Mother and Jack; I see love only. In school Zaida told me she couldn't wait to get married to get away from her parents. She said because I didn't have them as parents, I wouldn't know how bad they are. She said her mother called her a whore when she went to a party after school and that she might as well open up her thighs for all the men to fuck her. I felt sorry for her. She said her prince would come and get her. But when I think of a prince, I think of Mo and me on the horse riding away from my parents. I didn't want to tell Zaida that the prince might not come.

Whores have feelings, too. What do they say when they see their parents? How do daughters of prostitutes know what's wrong and right? I don't know if I'm ever going to tell anyone about Jack going into that house. What is it like to sleep with men for money? I tried to imagine it just by looking at men on the street for a day. I would imagine going upstairs with them, smelling their odors while I went up the dark stairway, looking at their clothes. But I couldn't even imagine kissing them. In my head, I couldn't touch them.

Mona would never think of these things.

Mother says to Mrs. King, "She's too young for that dress." And to me, "You're not getting it."

I know I am a woman.

Shame

The sound of water pulls my thoughts down from somewhere in the sky back to the bathtub.

Mona wanted to show me that she could open the
locked bathroom door. I was lying in the bathtub when
she opened the door laughing, and she saw me touching
myself. She couldn't see that I had my finger inside, but
she knew. She turned and closed the door, ashamed. Drew
touched me there one night when I was staying at her
house. She asked me if I had feelings when I touched myself there and I said yes. She asked if I would feel the same
thing if she touched me. I said I didn't know. She put her
hand under the cover and brought her hand under my
panties. I told her a little lower and she rubbed me with
slow and gentle movements. Then I told her to do it faster
and not to stop and then I breathed out. "It worked," I
said. She took her hand away, pleased with herself. I said
I wanted to do it to her now but she said no, she's
ashamed. It was unfair, I thought, but she turned her back
and fell asleep.

I wish Mo could see me come out of the shower with a white towel wrapped around my body, watch me cream my body, and comb my hair. I know Mother is going to say something about the lipstick and the dress. The two photographs on the desk look different. The woman with the thin upper lip in the photo album could have been my friend. The other photo is with Mo and Jack standing next to me. I imagine myself as the beautiful woman. I want to be her. The photos might look the same if I look at them long enough. I tear the one of myself and Jack and Mo into pieces.

Mo doesn't like little girls.

Blue Sweater

"I see what you mean," Jack says to Mother, when he sees the black dress that she got for me anyway. Mother's glittering dress looks like a frail Christmas tree. Jack's polo shirt is too tight and he's wearing the same pair of trousers that he always wears to parties. Mona is wearing beige pants and a loose top, and Peter has on a light brown baggy shirt and jeans. When we get in the car, Mona looks up at the moon. "It's a full moon," she says. "They say people act strange." She breathes in the warm night air, and I know she wants to keep the air inside her so she can remember Dar es Salaam for years later.

There are groups of Americans, Germans and Indians outside the inviting, acorn-colored lights of the Zebra Club. They walk inside in slow motion and their faces are bright with the well-fed glow that you see at these parties.

The doormen are wearing beige shorts, white polo tops and safari hats. They look like little boys who are about to go hunting.

Enzo and Mr. Porter wave to us and Mr. Porter looks at my dress as if he's seeing someone else. Enzo's hair is combed back and I can see his straight dark eyebrows better. The only thing that is strong about his face is his nose. It's long and strong. I don't like his mouth because it droops down a little. His wide V-shaped hairline on his forehead makes him look like nobility. "Nice," he says, looking at me.

We follow Enzo inside to our table and I look around for Mo. There's a live band that's playing "You Don't Bring Me Flowers" a little off-tune. The guests clap when the band finishes the song. Mother's hands come together, clapping without feeling. What would happen if my body was somehow connected to Mother's and she could only clap if I clapped? Siamese twins maybe feel that way forever. I wish I knew how it felt to be stuck to someone for so long.

Two Indian women speak English with a soothing accent that I have gotten used to. I will listen for these voices in London when I go back.

On the plane coming here, I thought if those stewardesses could see how ugly they looked with those blue and red flowered uniforms and those silly village hats, they wouldn't want to work for British Airways. Now I wish I could see myself from a distance and see who I am, or what I look like, or what I walk like. I don't dare get up because the dance floor is empty and everyone would look at me. There are four men standing next to the band talking, and I think I see Mo, but I can't tell. I lean my head a little to the right to see better, but it's no good. I get up to go toward the ladies. "Shall I come?" Mona says. We always go to the ladies' together. "No, it's OK," I say, walking in the direction where the men are standing. I can always turn to go to the ladies' if it's not him. As I pass the group,

I know it's him from the back, his hair, his shoulder and his voice. Pretending I haven't seen him, I go on.

In the mirror, the dress looks much shorter than it really is. My lips, my nose, my eyes all look so separate. I want to see myself talking so that I can see the way Mo might see me. I'm not going to eat. I don't want him to see me eat. I look ugly when I eat. I put on the lipstick Mother had put on, and I feel her lips on mine. Once, I lent Mother my blue sweater. She tried it on, put on her lipstick, and for one moment, when I walked into the room, I thought I saw myself there. In the mirror, I sometimes mistake her for me. I hear the band playing "Le Chic" before I rub my lips and leave the ladies' room.

"Hello, Tatum," Mo says. He doesn't say anything about the black dress.

I have to do something before my heartbeat gets faster. I'm old enough to ask for what I want and to do what I want. If he doesn't like it, then I don't care. I have to do something.

"Do you want to dance?" I ask him quickly. For one instant, I think I see him look at me carefully. He can't be scared of me. I have to act like a young girl so he's not scared.

"Enzo is getting the drinks for me." I fake my excitement at Enzo.

There's slow, jazzy music playing and people start dancing a kind of ballroom dance. The men hold one hand up and the other hand goes around the women's waist. Mo waves at Jack and shrugs his shoulder as we stand facing each other. I put my arms on his shoulders and we dance slowly. Just like in my daydreams, I look at his eyes and his ears. He looks over at Jack and Mother and Mona and Peter and says to me, "You've changed your hair."

135

"Yes, it's different," I say.

I look at his hairline. I want to remember everything.

"How are Mona and Peter?" What else can he ask?

"They are fine," I say.

"Good."

I think of all the things I want to say to him, and I can't catch the words that rush past me. I can't get them out of my mouth.

"Maybe I'll treat myself to London next year." Is he saying this to make me happy?

"What about your job?"

"I'm getting tired of it," he says, looking over at Enzo. "I might get a government job. But you have to have good connections to get it."

"What would you do?"

"Accounting, pushing paper, whatever they give me. I just don't like to wear suits and say 'Yes, sir, no, sir' every day."

"What would you love to do?" He thinks, then laughs. "Watch films. Any films." I laugh with him.

"Before Jack's brother died, I used to go to his house every afternoon after work. He was the only one in the neighborhood with a VCR and a TV. You would walk into his house, and it was packed with women and little children sitting on the floor watching Indian films."

"I've seen them in London."

"You know the ones where there's a good brother and a bad brother, and then there's a beautiful girl who comes to the city and the good brother saves her from the bad brother?"

"Yeah, and then they burst into song and dance. That was funny," I say.

"I like the songs and dances, it takes me to another world." We look at each other and smile.

Enzo comes over and the warmth of Mo's hand around my waist is gone. Mo walks to our table and Enzo's voice replaces him. "Can I have the pleasure?"

I don't say anything. We just dance till the song ends. Enzo likes the other song, too, and we dance on.

"You know what I like about you?" he says.

"What?"

"How indifferent you can be to people you feel indifferent about."

I laugh because he's so silly. "I'm not like that," I say. "I don't know what to talk about."

"What do you talk about with Mo?" he asks.

"It's just chatting," I say.

"You enjoy chatting with him?" I can't tell from the way he looks at me if he knows.

"I do."

"So let's chat," Enzo says. What he wants to say is something else and I wait for him to say it.

"OK?"

"You've changed," he says out of the blue. "You look so different tonight."

"I have makeup on." This is something that the woman in the novel would never have said. I don't know why I said it. She would have thought of something cool to say. But I don't need to be cool for Enzo.

"And you've painted your nails."

"Yes."

"And you've shaved your legs." He looks down at my legs. He wants to embarrass me.

"Please!" I say looking around us.

"Your dress is different, too. Are you going to be like this from now on?"

"Like what?"

"Like this." I want him to describe me like he sees me; then, maybe I'll know what Mo sees.

No one pays much attention to us when the music stops and we go back to the table. Only Jack is smiling at me. He thinks that Enzo and I like each other.

Enzo sits next to me at the table. Mo is on the other side between Mother and Peter. I look quickly his way but he's busy eating. He doesn't look my way once. Enzo watches me, and before I look away he crosses his eyes and blows out his cheeks.

"You're funny," I say.

"If you can't make girls love you, then make them laugh."

"So what do you do?"

"What's the question?" he asks.

"I mean how would you let them know?"

"You mean without making a fool of yourself?"

I say, "Not a fool. But to see if they like you."

He takes on a pose as if thinking about a very serious question. "It's difficult. Boys are different. I try being funny and then when they least expect it, I hit home."

"Like how?"

"Like I would say, for example, 'Tatum, that nail polish color stinks, but can I kiss you?'" I look at him and his eyes look serious. No one else seems to have noticed this. I'm shocked because he's not joking.

Then he says, "I guess not. You see, your reaction showed that you're not interested in kissing me, so I pretend that it was just a joke and I then wouldn't get hurt. You know, like the day after when people say, 'Well I was too drunk last night to know what I was doing.'"

He puts his fork on the side of his plate and says, "The 'but' sentences are the killers because you really have to be creative then."

Enzo is weird.

I hear one American woman saying to her friend, "I wonder what men feel when they get hit in the groin." An Indian woman tells a German woman that she knew a woman once who married her stepson without knowing it. Her ex-husband hadn't told her that he had a son from another marriage. After the divorce, she had met another man, married him, and when he took her to his father's house, she met her ex-husband.

The waiter fills everyone's wine glasses with a pinkish wine. Mona looks at me, and we both wait for the right moments in between the meal when everyone is talking to take some sips. No one notices that I am drinking wine. This is not the first time. I drank too much a few years ago at a party and felt sick. Everything was going round and round in my head.

The wine makes me feel good tonight; I feel like smiling all the time. My body is filled with a warm feeling. This is love. I have so much love in my body. I look at Mo and I want to be alone with him in one room and I want his hands on my breasts and his lips on my lips. He turns his head and I smile at him. He smiles back like he's my brother.

I hate him. I hate him for making me feel this way. I don't want to feel this way ever again. I can't think of anything. I'm not hungry and I don't eat anything, which makes Jack complain because he was telling Mo how he loves to watch me eat. I always show such pleasure when I eat. Jack boasts that he can eat anything any time of the day and that he has a cast-iron stomach. I feel heavy and light at the same time. Everything is in slow motion and I feel wet between my legs. It feels good.

I watch Mo's every move. He gets up to go to the rest room. I look around and when no one is watching, I pretend I have to go to the toilet. No one is paying any attention—they're watching the Greeks dancing together in a round group and making a lot of noise. I try and walk steadily to the bathroom and quickly wash my hands. I can see the men's door opening through the half-open door and I wait, drying my hands slowly.

He comes out and I rush out, pretending that I haven't seen him.

"I didn't see you," he says, going back to the table with me. I have to have him alone for just a few minutes. I have to be like a little girl asking for ice cream so that he thinks he can't say no. I say, "Let's dance," trying to keep all emotions out of it as if it's just a game or a bag of sweets I want.

We go to the dance floor, and I take a deep breath and put my arms around him and I feel his breath on my cheek. I bring my face closer to his and rub my hair against his lips. I don't know if he notices it or not, but he says, "Have you been drinking wine?"

"Yes."

"Aren't you too young to drink?"

"Don't you drink?" He doesn't say anything.

"I drank on my trip to Spain." I say. I want him to know that I'm not as young as he thinks. I want him to know that I'm a woman and that I love him.

He asks, "You were in Spain alone?"

"No, with my class," I say. He's so stupid, thinking that he can treat me like a girl. "We drank wine at night." I smile a little smile. "We would wait till the lights were off and we'd drink and smoke."

"You smoke?" I knew this would get him. I want to laugh out loud.

"Sometimes," I say.

140

"People's mouths stink when they smoke," he says. This is perfect, so I say, "Why, wouldn't you kiss a girl who smokes?" I like the way this sentence sounds.

He looks lost. "No. No, I don't think so."

I don't want him to think I'm just a girl flirting desperately with him. I want him to know. "I should remember that," I say quite seriously.

He looks as if he's thinking about what I just said, and he doesn't say another word. He just dances on, waiting for the music to finish.

"I don't think you should have any more to drink."

I feel brave and strong and powerful and he is so weak. Everyone is weak tonight. I can be anybody I want. I say, "Is that cologne? It smells nice."

"Aftershave."

"It smells good." I rub my cheek against his chin.

"Will you promise not to drink any more?"

"Why?"

"Because young girls shouldn't drink."

"I'm not a young girl."

"Well, a young lady shouldn't drink _or_ smoke."

"Why do you care?" There is silence. He doesn't know what to say. He's thinking of something. He says, "It's an unhealthy thing to do, for a smart and sweet girl like you."

I smile. I am smart and sweet. I'm going to think about this over and over. I don't even have to write it in my journal—I will remember it forever.

I ask him, "What's your dream woman like?"

"I don't have a dream woman."

"If you could choose one woman here, who would you choose?" What will I say if he says me? God, what will I say? I almost don't listen to his answer.

"I haven't really looked around."

"It doesn't really have to be 100 percent. Just near."

"I don't know." I love the way he says that. He sounds so innocent and honest.

"Come on," I say. "Anybody."

"I have to be able to talk to her."

"OK, from the women you've talked to then." I have to keep it up.

"I don't know that many women."

I take in a deep breath and rub the front of my thigh against his groin. He looks over my shoulder at Jack, who is too drunk to notice. Mo is scared. I feel a hard lump against my thigh. It's me that made him get hard. It's all because of me.

I say, "How about the Indian woman in London?" I can ask a lot more if I want to. He says, "I think we should go, Tatum."

I blurt out, "I like the way you call me Tatum." I regret saying that the minute it leaves my mouth. He looks at me and says, "I think your family is leaving."

"*Asante.*"

"For what?"

"For the dance," I say.

I walk as straight as I can without grinning. I want to laugh and breathe out. Mona's worried look makes me smile. She holds my elbow and we walk to the car together. I wish I could fly right now.

Back in my room I tape together the photo. My face looks so much better now, even attractive in a strange way. I like myself this way.

Words

If Mother was in a bad mood when I was in her womb, I might have grown up to be angry. If she had been angry and sad, I might have become just like her. With Mona she must have been kind and gentle.

The wine is making my head ache; it feels like it's going to burst. My body is light and tingly, and Mo is probably in bed asleep. I imagine myself rubbing against his warm body. I pace the room and think about what I'm going to do when I see him next. I am his "smart and sweet girl." I wish he would say it again and again in my ears. My heart is flying. I want to call him and tell him I loved every minute with him.

He wouldn't know what to say. It's late and I might wake his mother. But she's probably fast asleep. Maybe he's just arrived from the Zebra Club and is getting ready for bed. I want us to get ready for bed together, then I would help him get undressed.

I pick up the phone and think of the perfect thing I could say. "Hi," I say out loud to myself. "This is your smart, sweet girl." That's silly. I don't want it to sound planned. "Hi, I hope I'm not disturbing." I have to practice the words first. "I'm sorry for tonight. I didn't know what I was saying." No, I didn't do anything wrong. "Hi. I was drunk" sounds like I'm trying to excuse myself. Then maybe he would say, "Don't be sorry; you're a sweet girl," or even "You're a smart, attractive woman." God, if he said, "Can I see you tonight?" I would say, "I can't." And then I want him to come to me and make me change my mind. Force me to change my mind.

Jack's heavy cough in the bathroom interrupts my thoughts. He coughs as if his whole throat is coming out. The sound makes me shiver just imagining what is coming out of his lungs. I can hear him spit all his insides into the washbasin. Jack must have coughed when he was in the cubicle with a woman, on top of her, smelling her lipstick and perfume. I was so angry once that I went in the bathroom and said, "Can't you cough like a normal human being?" He shouted at me like he had never done before. And I went to my room and cried. I shouldn't care, I know, but I still cried because I was scared.

I have to do it. When Jack's throat noises are over, I pick up the phone and dial Mo's number. After the second ring he picks up. "Hello." I can't breathe. I can't move.

He says, "Hello, hello." I lean against the wall to stop myself from falling.

I can hear men's voices and music in the background. Mo's voice is different, louder and slurring. Maybe he's drunk. Some man's voice says, "Chickenshit, give that to me." I hang up.

I feel hot and weak. I can't believe that he's not lying in bed thinking of me. He's laughing with some men. He doesn't care.

"Damn it, damn it," I say out loud. So loud maybe Mona can hear.

I don't care.

I have to lose weight. I must stop eating. I want to be as skinny as Olivia Newton John. The *Cosmopolitan* on my desk tells me how to lose ten pounds in ten days. Mother says I shouldn't read all that rubbish in the magazines.

I'm lonely.

Barbra Streisand

"Tear off a small cluster of grapes, hold them in your hand and eat one grape at a time," Mother always says. "It's ugly to tear one grape away from a bunch when it's in the bowl." If I pluck Mo away from my head like the grapes, I will be ugly. I want to be somebody so that everyone will be proud of me and say, "Look, isn't she wonderful." I want Mo to think he was stupid for not having paid enough attention to me. That's what I want.

"Why are you dieting?" Mother asks me at dinner at the restaurant.

"I'm not. I like salad," I say.

Peter chuckles and says, "One look at her and you'll know."

Jack said I'm not fat and I have a beautiful body and I should be proud of it. I watch him staring at my body. Jack told us that he used to be thinner, but the wealthier he got, the fatter he became.

I want to be thinner. I want a smaller nose. I want fuller breasts and a smaller waist. I want to be like those girls you see on TV who live in California. Skinny, blonde, and on roller skates. I want to look like that.

"You could have had pasta or pizza. You love pizza," mother says.

Everything revolves around food. When Mother found out about Dad and Jennifer, she wanted to know what kind of lentils Jennifer used in her soup. We made sure to tell her that Jennifer's soup didn't taste good and she felt better.

Mother took us to see three films, one after the other, when she found out about them. She said that Dad was leaving us for good and she didn't know if he was going to come get us to live with him. I can only remember one film, with Barbra Streisand on a white piano. Mother held our hands tight in the street as if we would fly away like balloons when she took us from one cinema to the other. We sat through all the films, and when we came out, it was dark and we went home—no one said a word. Dad didn't come to get us, and I guess we just stayed with Mother after that. That night after the films, I dreamed that Barbra Streisand came to my bed and I called her mother; she stroked my hair and said everything would be all right.

Mona wasn't always skinny. In her older pictures she was pudgy. But something happened after she got those red rashes under her arms. I don't know what. She suddenly became thin and lovely in one night. The doctor said that it was stress related, and when I told her it must have been that film marathon with Mother, we both laughed.

She has a great stomach for bikinis. I have never worn a bikini in my life. I would die if Mo saw me in a bikini.

Peter is not into food. If it's there he eats it; if not, he doesn't. I don't think I've heard him say "hmmm" even once.

"Either she hates herself or she's in love," Peter says when my salad arrives.

Mother says, "Puppy love."

"Who?" Mona asks.

Mother puts a shrimp in her mouth and says, "Enzo."

Mother's thoughts are so funny, I want to laugh.

Mona looks at me lost and says, "Really?"

"Woof, woof," Peter barks in my ear.

I don't really care if they think I'm in love with Enzo, because I'm not. I don't want them to know about Mo. I don't say anything.

I wish right at this moment they would all disappear and I was here on my own and I could do whatever I wanted. I wish they would all go away from here. I wish they never existed. I wish they would leave me alone.

The lump in my throat makes me feel weak. I leave the table before I start to cry and pretend I have to go to the bathroom. Instead, I turn right and slip out on the sand and walk along the beach. A few minutes later, I feel Mother behind me. Her voice sounds smooth, almost like Barbra Streisand's. "What would you do if we just disappeared and left you alone?"

"I could do whatever I want."

"Like what?" She walks faster on the sand.

"I could be me."

Mother asks, "Who are you now?"

"I have to do what you tell me to." The smell of the ocean makes me dizzy.

"What's stopping you? You're free," she says.

"I can't do anything on my own. There's always someone there."

"We'll leave you alone." She says it as if she's so sure.

"I'm never going to be left alone." She doesn't answer. She just looks at the sky and then at the ocean. We walk on like this for some time. Mother appears almost normal with the moon shining on her hair.

I ask her, "Were you in love?"

After a while she says, "No."

"Why did you marry Dad?"

"I thought it was for convenience. There wasn't much choice. But I fell in love with him."

"Why did you divorce?"

"Before the divorce, a woman gave me the advice to always listen to my husband and be his slave, even if he has a mistress." Mother looks at the lights in the horizon. "And I looked at her; she was old and fat and her hair had fallen out."

I laugh and Mother strokes the back of my hair.

She says, "I thought, 'I don't want to end up like her.'"

I don't have anything to say. Her words don't really make sense but I listen.

"I wanted him to be with me only, but he was never there. I tried to hold on to him," she stops walking. "He just slipped away through my fingers, you know, like a slippery rope. I couldn't hold on to him."

"And Jack?" I ask.

"No."

"So why did you marry him?"

"When you don't have anything or anybody, you see someone strong and you think he'll take care of you." She stops and turns to look at me. "Then you think, if I do everything for him, everything will be fine. One day you wake up and they don't do the things you want them to, and then you think, I could have done this for myself."

I think, Would I ever marry Enzo and do everything for him, even if I didn't love him? I try to picture it and can't. Maybe you lose your self-respect when you get older. Why did she do it?

Her voice says, "I want you to be somebody. Do it for yourself first. Don't rely on men to take care of you. School is important," then, "I am proud of you."

She looks beautiful under the moon. I think she would be the perfect tourist who would stand in front of the building and marvel at it and wonder how it was made. Maybe Mother is someone different from the one I know. She's not just someone who sits in front of the TV watching old films about the ancient Romans.

She says something that makes me laugh so much I have to hold my stomach. "If I had known that Jack wears those special shoes to make him look taller and then takes the contraptions out at night, I don't think I would have married him."

We laugh so much that tears come to our eyes. Then we walk back to the restaurant.

"Remember that time when I read the name of those constipation pills you were taking?" I ask.

"And it had the same name as my cousin who was always constipated?" Mother says.

"Yeah, and we both laughed so much you had to go to the bathroom," I say.

"You've always been the one who really knew how to make me laugh."

I don't know what to say. I just want to listen to her talk. It's the same safe feeling I have when I watch clothes turn in the washing machine at home. Round and round, the clothes wash themselves in the warm, foamy water until they're squeaky clean.

The Tire

When Mother stands in the kitchen frying eggplants, she looks like she knows exactly what she's doing. Maybe she could cook all along and I just made up some story in my head that she couldn't. Thoughts make themselves up without me and then I believe them. If my thoughts get lost somewhere and I can't reach them, could I be dead? I will speak out everything in the air, so my thoughts can't go away; that way, maybe I can keep them inside me for a longer time. If I say my name out loud, I could stay in this world and not pretend that someone on TV is watching me, somewhere doing the same thing that I'm doing. I will hold on to my name every time I breathe. I will be myself and say my name out loud. I can pretend I'm in prison when I'm alone in my room, the only person left in the world. The world has only one room with me inside it. In my prison, with no one else there, I am free.

God, I feel so sick at having eaten so much chocolate in my room last night. I feel sick, and I can't even cry because being fat isn't something you cry about.

Enzo has come with us to the Kariakoo market today. A crowd is gathered around a woman who sings the *Taraab,* the traditional sung poetry that Mr. Porter made us listen to at his party. Peter and Enzo go to a *nyama choma* table where women prepare the barbecued meat on thin skewers. Everywhere there is a sign saying "Safari Lager," which, according to Peter, is pretty harmless. *Konyagi* is what Mo warned Jack about. He said it's a white-rum concoction that could kill you.

There's a crowd gathered around a man sitting under the clock tower carving black figures out of big pieces of trees. He is surrounded by shiny black figures whose faces sit there, waiting. There's one statue with the shape of a woman kneeling on the tree with little children clinging to her. The children are climbing all around her. Her whole body is made of children up to her neck. Her face looks like a man's. The child that I like most is the small one holding on to the mother's breast. Another one holds on to her arm and the other is climbing up her thigh. They are all so stuck together that if you could take one away, the other ones would fall to pieces. They are glued together forever. Someone said that women in Africa show their breasts because they have something to say; it's a sign of protest.

Enzo says he would love to have a crowd around him like that man.

"What do you think of Salim?" Mona asks when we get back to the house. This is the first time she has asked me what I think about someone else.

"He's so bony," I say. I don't know what else to say.

She says, "Yeah. You know, he doesn't even look at us."

"He looks at you."

"No, he doesn't," she says. "Anyway, he's not old."

She sees through all my secrets because she watches me. "I was drunk."

"No, you weren't," she says. "What did he say to you?"

"That I shouldn't drink and that I was smart and sweet."

I can't say anything about love because she would think I'm stupid. "He's OK."

"You're fourteen." She makes it sound as if she is saying it for the first time.

"I'll be fifteen." I could have said I want to put away his clothes and comb his hair. If I was his wife, then Mother and Dad and maybe Jack would come by and visit us and tell us what a beautiful house we had and I could look after his mother and be nice to her.

Or that I want to be like those couples on TV when the man goes to work and kisses his wife and children. They all look so happy together.

It's a shame I can't watch TV here. I don't feel like thinking anymore.

What if this happy family thing is just a big lie? I told Ella once that my parents were divorced and she said, "So?" I thought she would be ashamed or at least feel sorry for me. She wasn't even surprised. She didn't even ask if I suffered—nothing.

Mona's friend Trish was dramatic when I told her. She said, why didn't Mona tell her herself, and when I asked Mona she said it wasn't important. I don't like Trish because she says the opposite of what I say.

I guess I didn't really suffer. Nobody says that they're proud of me, not even for the suffering. Maybe they say it when I'm not there. And I can't remember being with Dad anyway, so I couldn't have really missed not having him around. Peter says all he remembers was holding his ears when Mother screamed and clung to Dad's leg, while he dragged her on the floor. "Don't leave," I think that's what she must have said. Peter says he never cried because he knew Dad was going to leave us anyway.

I could never scream like that.

Standing on the balcony, I can see him coming. Mo is coming to get Jack to go to Mr. Porter's. He doesn't see me. I can watch as long as I want. I wish he would look up and see me in my white nightgown. I wish he would just look up. Maybe he sees me but doesn't let it show. I will never tell anyone if he sees me now, not even Mona.

Maybe if I were a photograph in a picture frame or a character in a book, he would look. I wouldn't leave the frame because I would be somebody else's picture. Sitting on the mantelpiece with shining eyes, I could listen to people talk. Then there would be no dried crust on the inside of my eyes when I wake up, and I wouldn't think of my breasts showing through my nightgown.

The air at night smells of dead meat. Africa is so dusty, no one would believe me if I told them. In London I saw a crowd on the news in South Africa that put a tire around a woman's neck and set it on fire. I saw the dust around her and the different-colored shirts worn by the men. She just sat there on her knees in the dust and looked up at the sky. I was so angry, angry at the men, angry at the women watching and angry at the cameraman that they didn't do anything to save her. I looked at the sky with her until she swayed from side to side and fell.

Angels

When Mona and I walk, it's against the traffic. Mona walks faster when she talks fast. Then I have to tell her to slow down because I get a pain in my side. Her minutes aren't wasted like mine. She talks because her minutes count. Even when she doesn't do anything, she still fidgets, like Mother who always has to do something with her hands. She says that I'm too slow at everything. I can't imagine Mona ever painting a picture.

Mother said, "What for?" when I told her I want to write something, anything. She said there were so many books in libraries and bookstores already. I imagined rows and rows of books in libraries and thought of my book being one of them.

Sometimes I think I want to lose my voice forever and wear sunglasses all the time. I wish I could ask Mona what to do. I wish I could ask her how I could stay here with Mo.

"Is Salim your boyfriend?" I say quickly.

She looks at me with her stern eyes. "Tatum, please."

We step over the brown pieces of palm leaves that have fallen on the street. Mona never tells me anything in detail. I always have to guess with her.

There's a man standing by a coconut tree selling coconuts. He has a monkey on his shoulder that fidgets. The man holds a huge, sharp knife in one hand and a green coconut in the other. He wears sunglasses. I can't tell if Mona is scared when he starts talking.

"Coconut juice?" he asks.

Mona says, "Yes, please."

The man sends the monkey up the tree. It twists the coconut round and round and then, holding it, comes down the tree with the coconut. The man pierces the fruit first, giving it to us to drink. Then he crushes it and gives us each a piece of the flesh. He takes our money and holds it in his hand until we walk away eating the flesh.

"Do you think Mother would let us stay here longer?" I ask her.

"Never."

"Why not?" I ask.

"Because," she says, meaning it's common sense. "She wants to see what we're doing."

I ask, "So?"

"So, you think she's going to let us stay here on our own?"

The hot, sticky asphalt pulls at my sandals. I look back at the coconut man next to the single tree sticking up against the sky. He stands there like a shadow with his monkey on his shoulder.

"Never," Mona says. If only I could stay here on my own, then Mo would take me seriously.

We turn and walk back the same way we came—on the beach instead of the road. Sand is better to walk on than asphalt. Asphalt doesn't change however many times you walk on it. I want Mona to be asphalt. I want her to stay Mona forever.

The coconut man is still there. I feel sorry for him today, because today it's my sorry day. But sometimes it changes to hate. Like the time I saw a woman eating at a restaurant on her own and I felt sorry for her. But then I hated her because she ate loudly and slurped her coffee and looked greedily at her food. Sorry and hate days are the days that I'm loneliest.

There's one hate day that I remember often. It even comes up in the middle of my daydreams. Mona and I went to our first party together without Peter. We entered the flat. The music was very loud and the rooms were all empty.

Three or four small rooms were dark. Some large lamps stood at the corner of each room. Nobody was there. It was a loud party, but no one had come. I asked Mona if we were the first people, and she said she thought so. We strolled with the music from room to room. There was a tall, blond boy standing in one corner looking at nothing in particular, and I knew I hated him. Then we went to another room. I don't remember how full it got later, but I remember the boy that I hated for no reason. Some days, when it comes up in my head I think maybe I just dreamed it and we never went to that party.

I hated the oil painting in our school in London, too. The long assembly hall and the pictures of dead men who were our headmasters.

It's all far away now.

Jack is on the terrace reading the paper. He has a mug of coffee and cookies in front of him. I don't think he will ever stop eating. I sit down on the floor next to him, and Mona sits in the chair next to him.

"Will they let me back in England if I have malaria?" I ask.

"You don't have it anymore," Jack says, sipping his coffee. He puts away his newspaper and looks out on the humid and calm afternoon.

"I know, but if I still had it?"

"We'd stay till you get better."

"But what if you had to go back?" Mona asks.

"We'd find a way," he says, turning to me. "Have you tried the mangos I bought you?" I'm the one he buys food for. Mother once said that if it weren't for me, they would probably all starve.

I nod remembering the hard, sweet taste of the stringy mango I shared with Mona.

Does Mona wake up in the mornings wondering why no one buys mangos especially for her? I'm stuck with myself and won't know what Mona feels like when people pay attention to her little sister instead. Mona gets up and goes to the kitchen.

"Did your parents let you stay in places on your own?" I ask Jack. His parents weren't living when he married Mother. He showed me their photograph in one of his albums. It was an old black-and-white photo of a man standing and a woman sitting. The man had Jack's lips and he was resting his hands on the woman's shoulder. Both were looking stiffly at the camera.

"See that building over there?" Jack points to an old house that is so far away it looks like a toy. "That's where I had my first you-know-what with a woman." He looks at me expecting a response. I just smile. I know everything about him. In London, he used to disappear for three or four days and come back looking tired and hung-over. With a whisky breath, he used to pull me aside and tell me about the money he'd won and then lost at the casino.

I say, "What's in that old colonial building in the town center?"

"Which one?"

"The one with the red curtains and the women outside."

Jack pretends to think.

"I saw you go in there." I'm not going to tell him that the woman forced me to go in there.

"What do you think it is?"

"Whorehouse."

"No, no, no." He doesn't seem to be nervous. "It's a place where you can just drink and listen to music."

"Oh."

I don't hear Mother coming, but she says, "What are you talking about?" Mona stands behind her. She has a pair of scissors in her hand, and she cuts the yellow parts of the leaves in the pots on the terrace as if she had been doing it all day and had been interrupted by Jack's statement.

"How old were you the first time?" I ask, changing the subject.

"Fourteen, fifteen maybe," Jack says, picking up a cookie.

Mother says, her back to us, "That's impossible."

Jack looks to the ground at the newspaper. "There's a lot of things you don't know."

"I know everything about you, but I just ignore it." Mother turns her head to him and looks at him straight in the eyes.

"What were you doing here at fourteen?" Mona asks Jack.

Mona doesn't really talk to Jack. She usually listens to him talk and then walks away. It's strange hearing her ask a question so direct.

"My family's first trip abroad was here," he says, looking in his coffee mug. "My father was posted here, so I had my first hanky-panky right here in Dar es Salaam," he says, winking at me. "And I've come back ever since."

"That poor girl wouldn't recognize your fat belly now," Mother says with a huff.

"Did your parents let you stay out late?" I ask.

"Let me? They couldn't control me."

Mother looks at Jack, doing her head shake so subtle, telling him not to talk. But we're used to it by now. She does the same thing when Jack watches films that Mother thinks we shouldn't watch.

She thinks that just because she's always around, we can't do what we want to do.

Mother looks so small standing there with the scissors in her hand. She looks like an angel. I want to buy her mangos.

Samosas

Samosas are magic food. They are crisp on the outside and spicy and mixed up on the inside. However much you try, you can't tell what's inside. Maybe a pea here, or a small piece of carrot there, but the pieces don't tell you what's in the samosas really. It doesn't matter how many you eat or if you watch how they're made; they're too mysterious to become boring.

Sitting in the courtyard, Mona and I can't wait to taste the samosas. Peter and Enzo went to the Kilimanjaro Hotel. The hotel is in the middle of Dar es Salaam's town center and looks like a high-rise office building. Its pool and bar are popular with the tourists. Mona says they go there to talk to the American girls they meet by the pool. I ask her where Salim is, and she says, "How should I know?"

The Patel family who invited us for lunch aren't the only ones who live here. The whole courtyard is surrounded by rooms or flats, and children run in and out of doorways and through colorful cloths hanging over invisible doors. Indian men lie on bright rugs and chew on seeds that make their tongues turn red. Some fetch water from a pump where women in saris are washing clothes. The women seem to be working by themselves, but somehow their work is in harmony.

Mona and I sit on a concrete block that surrounds the yard with steps leading down to the main courtyard. Jack sits on a chair that makes him look like he's leaning back, next to Mr. Patel. Mother is trying conversation with some women who are sitting next to the other women making samosas. She asks questions but is having difficulty understanding the answers.

A group of colorfully dressed women sit around an open stove that has a huge wok on it. It looks just like Chinese woks. The shiny saris wrapped around the women's bodies glisten in the sun. I don't know why they don't sweat in the African heat and can still sit in front of the fire like that.

Heavy with years of pride, a woman droops her shoulders as she makes little shapes of pastry on a wooden board. Two other women take the pastry from a thin-layered heap and, holding it in one hand, scoop a handful of the magic filling. They close it by wetting it with water on one side and press the pastry gently. They work so delicately, you might think it's going to break any minute. A carved silver tray holds the tall heap of samosas before they are put in the oil. The creamy hill looks as fragile as a newborn baby. One woman picks each samosa up and gently lets it slip from her hand into the boiling oil. Another woman stirs the oil slowly with a large metal spoon with holes.

The smell of samosas cooking in the oil makes me so hungry I want to ask them for one. The woman with the spoon takes the crisp, brown samosas and puts them on the brown pile that is building on her right.

Mona swallows her saliva and stares at the brown, grown-up samosas. She is just as hungry as I am. Mother didn't let us eat much because she said we would ruin our appetite for lunch. We look like we haven't eaten for days.

"I don't think we can have one, do you?" I ask Mona.

She looks at the pile of crisp, brown samosas. "I don't know."

What Mona says is different from what she wants to do. She doesn't do things she wants, and this makes me bolder than her.

"They're not giving anyone any," I say, my mouth watering. Maybe the women had so much to eat that they're not eating the samosas; otherwise how could they just sit there and not eat a single one?

Mona says, "They're counting them."

She turns to see where Mother is. Mother can't tell if we're hungry. Jack looks over to us and nods.

Then Mona asks, "If you want it hard enough, you'll get it?"

When I see Mona getting up and going toward the women, my heart beats faster although I know exactly what she's going to do. I can't say anything. The women watch Mona as she goes to one of the women, picks up two samosas, smiles, says thank you and walks back to me. They watch her glow in silence. She smiles as she hands me one and keeps the other one for herself. It's the same smile she had when Jack told her that he is proud of her when he sees that she is not so shy. The hot samosa burns my mouth, and the dusty women laugh as Mother looks at us, embarrassed. Mona notices Jack's smile. Then she starts humming as she eats the samosa.

"That was good," I say.

"The truth?"

"Yes." I'm glad she is my sister.

The spicy women, not having eaten a single one, put the samosas in bags and then in boxes. They arrange some on a tray. Mother says they sell most of them to shops.

Mrs. Patel gets up and opens one of the curtains in the courtyard and says that lunch is ready. Past the curtain is a secret cave with big, soft cushions. There is a table in the middle of the room that has been set as if by magic. It has rice and colorful curries and sauces. There are *bajias* and thin, fried, crisp hot bread and yogurt. The tray full of samosas sits in the center like a seasoned hill in a painting. I wish Mo could see this. I want to eat with Mo, I want him to feed me. I want to drink from the same glass as him. That would make me happy. I wish he would think about me from the moment he wakes up until he goes to bed. I don't want to think up stories about him anymore. I want it to be real.

Mother motions to me that I should try the brown lamb stew.

"Try the lentils," Jack says. Mona takes some lentils and then gives me the bowl. The mellow air in the room smells of curry and incense. Everyone is so busy putting food on their plates that for one instant, I think they have forgotten each other. It reminds me of the time Jack and I went to a Chinese restaurant in Soho. I was invisible. People looked through each other as if they were looking through glass. The waiter didn't have a pad to write on when we ordered. He would just nod his head and say "uh," "uh," "uh."

The lentils move down my throat, forcing me to swallow them. Chewing slowly, I imagine what it is doing to my body. What would it be like if we ate grass like the cows do? How does hay feel between horses' teeth, or what do camels feel in their jaws when they are chewing? Once I saw a snake swallowing a whole egg on TV and then spitting out the shell afterwards. That night, I went to the kitchen and stared and stared at an egg until I felt I knew what it felt like to swallow one. What about a live mouse? I don't want to eat anything that lives. I don't want to eat anything that used to live.

"Try this." Jack hands me the lamb stew. I imagine the blood and the warmness draining from the lamb's neck. I imagine the lamb weak, falling to the ground.

"No, thank you, I don't eat meat," I say.

Mother looks up and Mona looks puzzled.

"Since when?" Mother asks.

"Since now," I say.

"Don't be so ridiculous," she mumbles.

"Hindus are vegetarians too," Mr. Patel says.

His wife says, "That's right."

I don't want my body to feel something dead inside it. Then it would mean that I'm dead and I don't want to die. I don't ever want to die.

The Flowers

Africa is red, yellow and orange, and if you can't find these colors, you can always bump into them on a man's T-shirt, a woman's yellow head scarf or an old man's orange scooter. The ocean at sunset is orange and dark brown, making the water look like it's on fire. Mother had a shiny yellow-orange silk scarf she used to wear when she went shopping on Oxford Street. This is what the water looks like at sunset. The boats on the ocean have been stretched so long, they look like dark brown shadows of men standing on tiptoe. The men might lose their balance, but they can't fall because they are glued to the boat.

When you look at the map of Africa on an atlas, you can't see any of this. It's just the shape of a woman's head yawning, with lines around it that mark borders with their different shades of geography-class green and yellow. You can't find the atlas-yellow and -green in Dar es Salaam, because they make these colors only for textbooks. Now that

I'm here, I don't want to draw maps and lines and fill them in with crayons anymore.

I write down things that I want to remember. But I won't write down things that I know I'll never forget. Like the time I danced with Mo and I felt his hard lump. I wrote in my journal that I had nothing to write because I will never forget it anyway. I want to read out loud the things I've written, but I don't want to hear myself saying it. "He put his hand on my forehead"; "He called me smart and sweet today"; "He plays cards next door most of the time"; "He doesn't want me to drink; that might mean that he likes me"; "I want to kiss him." Suddenly, I turn around and see Peter standing behind me looking down on my diary. I get so scared I start to hiccup. He starts to laugh, holding his stomach. He points to the phone and says, "Pick up, it's Dad." I blush because I don't know if he heard me whisper sentences out loud.

He will probably go downstairs and tell everyone that he scared me so much that I had to hiccup. He might have thought it was just a book I was reading to myself. There is silence on the line when I pick up the receiver.

"Hello, hello!" I don't care whether Dad has hung up or not. Careless, like the man I saw one night sitting along the freeway staring at the cars speeding past. He just sat there and looked as if he had been there for years. Those cars drove by fast and the man just sat there staring at them.

Dad's unreal voice says, "So now we can talk."

"About what?" I ask.

"You called me, remember?" he says.

"Yes," I tell him.

"Are you all right?" his voice sounds worried. I think of all the things I want to do that Mother won't let me.

"I can't go where I want to. I can't stay where I want to," I say.

"What do you want to do?" he asks.

"I want to stay here longer, but Mother won't let me."

"She's right," Dad says.

"Why? I could stay with our neighbors, or Jack has so many friends here. I could stay with them."

"No," he says simply.

"You think something is going to happen?"

"You're a girl and you're too young to stay at anyone's house."

"You think I couldn't do it when Mother's around? If people really want to do things, they do it if the parents are there or not." I can't say *sex* or anything but Dad knows what I mean by *it*. There's silence on the other side and he doesn't say anything.

"Who are these friends Jack has over there?" he asks.

"Families with children," I say. "Will you talk to Mum?" I ask, "Please, Daddy." I can imagine his grin on the other side when I call him that.

"No," he says.

"Please, Daddy."

"I said no."

I don't want to think of leaving here without kissing Mo. I have to stay.

"Did you send money?" Let him think that Mother has changed me so much that I care about him sending money.

"Of course." Now he doesn't have anything to say. "Well, say hello to everyone. I kiss you."

"Bye," I say.

One day, when he was supposed to pick me up from school, he came late. Everyone had gone home and I sat on the steps and waited. I thought he had forgotten. But he finally came. Driving back home, he pressed the buttons of the car windows down and said, "Can you smell it?" I said, "What?" and he said, "The blossoms," inhaling the air. "Every time I drive past here in the summer, I can smell the flowers." He said, "Can you smell it?"

"Yes, it's nice." And then we drove home.

Soup

Reading a book is like eating. You can only read so much, and then you have to put it away. And when you're full you have to wait. Then when you get hungry, you read again. Sometimes, I just like to look at the alphabet, and sometimes I'm jealous of it. Every letter has a character of its own. The letter *C* is the helpful nun that protects *B* and *D*. *H* is a coward and *L* is the traitor who has crossed over the border to *M* and *N*. I'm the letter *T* who is hissed at by *S* or gawked at by *U* and made fun of by *Q*. I want to be an *A* or *Z*, nothing in the middle. The alphabet makes my mind wander.

The same thing happens when I eat. My thoughts are all over the place when I'm eating, and when I finish, I see that I haven't tasted the food at all. Soup is boring because you just spoon the food into your mouth without thinking. And anyway, it's for sick people. With pizza, I'm always there. If you eat with your hands, you have to concentrate on the cheese and get it in your mouth so you don't look bad. If you use a knife and fork, then you have to think how to cut it. With pizza, I can't daydream. If I have dinner with Mo, it will be pizza.

Jack breathes so heavily through his nostrils when he eats that you would think he was an animal that has been starved. He doesn't use napkins, either, and sometimes he eats with his mouth open.

Mother eats with her head down. She brings her head down to the food and her eyes look at the tablecloth. And when she eats, she has the same sad expression on her face like she has with everything else. Except when she doesn't like the food, then she will complain and push her food aside. If she's hungry and doesn't get her food on time, she will be in a bad mood until it comes. I think Mother changed or I did, and I can't see her as Mother but some child. Now I think back and try to remember when that was. At night, sometimes, when I want to put my head on her chest and let her stroke my hair, I think of her eating and nothing makes sense. She could try and play like those mothers on TV who go up to their daughters' room and tell them what to do. Maybe if she thought about eating, she might be Mother again.

Mona eats fast. She's in a hurry when she eats and sometimes talks with food in her mouth. Peter makes noises and I can hear him chewing from a mile away. Jack says he likes eating with me because I eat like a princess. I just pretend someone is filming me and my film is being shown all over the world and everyone is watching. Once I saw myself eat in the mirror, and it was all wrong. After that, I practiced every day till I knew my back was straight; with my head up, I brought the food to my mouth instead of my head down to the food. Now I know how to eat right.

American actors eat so nice, but never in real life. Men in real life eat with their mouths open.

Sitting by the pool at the Kilimanjaro Hotel, Peter bites into an apple, making noises. I am trying to read and I can't concentrate.

Peter has this color brochure advertising a casino. The photos show rich men in tuxedos and women in evening dresses. In each picture the men are playing a game, and the women lean over the table with their hands on the men's shoulders, their breasts inviting the men to come play with them.

"What's it about?" Peter asks me about the book I'm reading, while signaling to the white-gloved man at the bar. The man has on a white suit and a black bow tie.

"A woman who plots to kill her husband to get to his money," I say.

"Nice thing for you to read," he says, taking a sip from some cocktail he has ordered. Ever since he turned eighteen, he stopped drinking beer in secret; now he only orders cocktails in public. The man comes to Peter in quick strides.

"Well, he was with another woman," I say.

"That's women for you," he says and orders some French fries.

"She's beautiful; she's smart," I say. "I don't know why she wants to kill him."

"Human nature." Peter likes to act like a cool millionaire who can afford anything.

"Maybe she's not happy being a housewife," I say.

"I want to be rich because women like that," Peter says.

"No, they don't."

"A woman who sees a man—let's take Jack—who has a lot of money and someone who's just working at a warehouse like Mo. Who is going to go for Mo?"

"Mo isn't poor."

"He isn't rich, either." Peter says.

"He has a nice personality."

"The point is, money attracts," he says impatiently.

"I want to buy my own things anyway," I say.

"I bet you the day I drive around in a convertible, I'd get more girls than Mo." He talks as if girls are stupid.

I don't care if Mo doesn't have any money. I would live in a small house with him in the middle of nowhere.

Enzo and Mona wave at us from the bar. They're both wearing straw hats they bought from the market.

When they come over, I hear Mona saying, "I don't know what Mo did in London."

"I'm talking reality here," Peter says. "Girls like men who have money, aren't I right?" he asks them.

"If you actually believe in it," Enzo says. "It might come true."

"Peter pretends he's Superman," Mona says. "One day he'll really believe it."

I read somewhere that if you really want something, then nothing can stop you from getting it. I think of all the things I could do to make Mo want me.

"Who wants fries?" Peter asks.

Daydreaming isn't enough. I can't daydream about Mo forever. If I want it to be real, I have to give up the dreaming.

The Bar

In the 1870s, Christian missionaries came from Europe to Tanzania and built schools and churches. This is what Peter told us before we set out on his "planned" route through Dar es Salaam and the surrounding villages. This is the first time that we're together like this—Jack, Peter, Mona and I. Usually it's Jack and me, or Jack and Mona, or Peter and Mona, but not like this. There is a strange silence in the Jeep. Jack and Mona don't talk much. Peter and Jack talk only if they have to, and Mona and Peter talk serious stuff. Mother didn't come with us; she said she needed a rest from the heat.

"What are we going to eat?" I ask. All the way, Peter has been boasting about this day trip without mentioning food.

"Planning a trip is difficult stuff," he says. "Anywhere we feel like it."

"Do you have any idea where we're going?" Jack asks, looking around. It's his turn to drive.

Peter looks at the map and says carefully, "When we get to Kasama Beach, make a right."

"There are no street signs here," Mona says. "You think there's going to be a sign saying Kasama Beach?" I giggle. Peter has the map but he doesn't know where we are because there are no signs.

If they had all the time in the world, then people wouldn't care where they were going. On the way there, they might find nicer places and stay awhile. Maybe places are a big deal because we think we have to get there on time. If we could live forever, then maybe Mother wouldn't rush me. She wouldn't tell me to go to school and get a good job because I could change my mind and do whatever I felt like and not care because I would never die.

Jack stops the car when we reach a village. Huts made of brown, hard mud with roofs of dried palm leaves woven together have the same color as the ground, which makes them look as if they have grown out of the earth. One small concrete building with a wavy aluminium roof has a concrete slab with a wooden bar on top. A sign in front says "*Iwanga*." A man standing behind the bar hands out cold beers from a refrigerator to some men who are standing around. There is music coming out of a tiny radio on the bar. They turn to look at us when we get out of the Jeep.

"There is actually a bar here!" Mona says.

Jack smiles and says, "Good."

"I mean this tiny place actually has a bar?" Mona says it again. If somebody asks her, "What was Africa like?" she would say, "They actually had a bar in this tiny village."

On our left, some women cook on an open fire with huge metal pots that look like the ones in cartoons where cannibals, with bones tied to their hair, stir people. Containers made of the same mudlike earth as the huts are stuck in the ground. What is the use of containers if you can't move them? Nearby are baskets that have the same form as the pots. Children with clear angel eyes peek at us behind their mothers' dresses. They giggle, bringing both hands up to their mouths. We walk over and order some Cokes. Jack and Peter get millet beer and we sit on one of the steps next to a hut.

Jack points to a white house with a thin, gold cross on its triangular, tin roof. The church looks like an oversized hut. It's white with red, blue and black triangles. The men at the bar don't seem to care much that we're here. Jack points to the church. "See the triangles there?" He takes a sip of his beer and says, "The triangle stands for food and life and the Catholic Trinity." He talks as if he knows all this. "Black stands for the people of Africa. Blue is the color of Lake Victoria, and red for fire and life."

He puts the empty beer bottle back on the bar, and we follow him toward the church. Nobody takes out the camera. Maybe because it's like the map thing—you can put your finger on places you've been and trace the lines of the country, but the colors, the smells, the sounds are not there. I don't want to take pictures of children sitting on twisty dead trees and say, "I was there," because either you're there or you're not. Inside the empty church, the altar looks like a stage. The back wall is painted light greenish blue. There is a long, rectangular table draped with a yellow cloth barely covering the front. Blue, red, white and black triangles on the floor. A colorful rug hangs behind it. Even the table legs are triangles laid on their side. Jack tells us about the tabernacle to the far right: "This is where the symbolic body of Christ lies." It looks like a man-made beehive. It's got a triangular roof with small, red triangles cut into it. In the middle is a copper shield that looks like a tortoiseshell. Two gold vases hold orange, fleshy flowers on either side.

Outside, girls with light pink and yellow dresses stand in a crowd of men in light blue trousers and shirts. The priests are in white except for the large red collars and skirts. The one who bears the cross is in a blue skirt.

"It's been a month already," I say. I want to be with Mo, but I'll be leaving soon. I feel like crying and screaming and holding on to him and telling him how much I love him. I don't want to go.

Mona says, "I can't believe it."

Black men in heavy, white robes sit around a large rectangular stone that looks like a tombstone.

"Going back is the dread," Peter says with a sigh.

"With bad notes, I would dread it, too," Jack says.

The large yellow candles are all lit around the grave. To the left is an open pavilion. A man dressed in white plays on two huge drums that are held on a piece of wood that looks like a catapult.

I say, almost too loud, "I don't have to go back. I don't have college," thinking maybe Jack will let me stay.

"We're all going whether we have to or not," Jack says. "Anyway, you're getting your notes soon."

The group around the church follows a man wearing thick glasses and a tigerskin shawl over his shoulders. Two black boys in choirboy robes are holding a Bible and a candle each. The red, green, yellow, blue and white procession floats by us silently, kicking dust. None of us say anything for a while. The drums get louder and louder.

Suddenly I think of something; I could make a bet with Jack.

"I failed economics." I know what he's going to say. But Mona says it first. "You don't know yet."

"I know," I say confidently.

Peter says, "Swots never fail."

"Well, this time I will," I say.

"I'm glad you're so optimistic," Jack says.

"I could bet on it," I say.

Peter says, "I'll bet with you."

I say, "No, I want to bet with Jack."

Jack looks at me and pats me on my shoulder and says, "OK, fifty."

I say, "No."

"Dishes for three weeks." Mona offers an alternative for him.

"No," I say. Jack knows I want something even better. This has made him even more curious.

"So choose," he says.

I want to say it quickly but not too quick. As we walk back to the Jeep, away from the dwindling church procession, I say, "If I'm right, I want you and Mum to let me stay here a week longer."

Peter just gives out a little breath, and Mona studies Jack's expression.

He sits behind the steering wheel and has already decided. "Something else," he says.

"What?"

"We can't do that; choose something else," he says.

He must have a better answer. Otherwise, he is admitting that he doesn't have a say in our family. It's Mother who makes the decisions. "Why can't you?" I can tell he is uncomfortable saying it. He says, "Your mother, for one."

Mona looks at me as if to say, "You're so naive. She'd never ever let you stay," she says.

"Why won't you?" I ask Jack; it's his decision.

Peter says, "Mother doesn't trust you."

"She doesn't trust other people," Mona adds.

I have already rehearsed this. "I could live at our house. Mr. Porter is next door."

"You can't live in the house alone," Jack says.

"Well, then I can move in one of Mr. Porter's rooms."

"With Enzo there," he says. "I don't think so."

"It would be a present from you if I pass. The best present you have ever given me." This will make him feel better. "There must be somewhere I can stay."

"I wouldn't even try it," he says impatiently.

Tonight will be the last night I will see him. I'm going to see the rooms he lives in, where he eats, where he sleeps. We're going to Mo's house tonight and I can't wait.

Staying

I'm never going to forget this. Like a photograph, all the details will be kept in a frame in my head. Then, to remember him, I will take out the photograph, with its faded colors, blow away the dust and remember the staircase, the hallway, the kitchen, the bathroom and his room—everything. My head must be empty before we leave for dinner at his apartment. I will let things fill my head slowly.

From the street, you can see Mo's curtains, Mo's lampshade and the top of his wooden cupboards. Mo moves from one room to another; I can tell from his walk. Mother's voice has turned into just a murmur beside me. I should be the last to go in, or should I be the first? Mother follows me and the others up the stairs. The light brown color of the walls and the darkness of the staircase give off warm heat. I watch Mo shaking hands with everyone. He doesn't see me. Finally, he shakes my hand and says, "Hi, Tatum. How are you?"

"Fine, thank you."

He turns and leads the way to the kitchen.

His mother doesn't speak English. She nods her head with an embarrassed smile and goes about her work in the kitchen. She wears a head scarf with big purple and red patterns on it. Within a few minutes, no one notices her anymore. She goes about her work like she's invisible. I try to see anything in her that would remind me of Mo. But she could be anyone's old mother working in the kitchen. There is no similarity at all.

"Let me show you the rooms and we can start dinner," Mo says. I don't know if he's embarrassed of his home. He shows us his mother's room, the tiny bathroom, the kitchen, a spare room and his room. He doesn't turn the lights on in the rooms. With just the shadows, I'll have to imagine what it's like inside when I go back home tonight. Mo turns on the light in the spare room. Everyone peeks in and walks away. I stay there longer and imagine myself inside—my nightgown on the bed, my bag on the chair, my clothes hanging in the closet.

"That's it. That's how I came back and stayed," Mo's voice says.

Everyone has already taken their seats at the table. Mo's mother has set the table with colorful Indian dishes so fast I think time went by while I stood still.

"I think it's very nice of you to stay here," Mother tells Mo, taking a sip from the yogurt drink next to her plate.

"Mo is a saint," Jack says. Mo is like his little brother.

"Whose room is that?" I ask, pointing to the spare room.

"That's the guest room," Mo says.

"You have a lovely home," Mother says.

"Not as lovely as yours." Mo doesn't even look at me once. Peter talks about how nice it must be to live right in the middle of Dar es Salaam, and Mona asks whether it's loud or dangerous at night. I don't even want to remember what everyone says. Dinner goes by in a haze.

"Thank you for everything you've done for us, Mo. You have to come visit us in London," Mother says.

What if he came? Would I think of him in London? Would I want to kiss him if he came?

Mo's mother serves a huge bowl of dessert. It is thin vanilla pudding with raisins in it. I take in the fresh and spicy taste with all the details I need for my dream tonight—the position of the rooms, where the kitchen is, where the windows are and how the curtains are drawn, so that when I dream of him, I will have the stage ready.

Now that it's time to leave, I wish I had paid more attention to what he said.

I would do anything to be alone with him in his room. I know I will never see him again. At the door I say, "Goodbye. Thank you."

He says, "It was a pleasure."

The moon has made the streets bright and shiny, and the heat in the air is out to strangle me. I want to breathe out the sadness and tell Jack to let me stay. I walk next to Jack holding on to his arm because I know he likes that.

"Isn't that house with the red curtains a few blocks away?"

Jack turns back quickly to make sure no one heard me.

"I don't want you to mention that again."

"Why? Did you do something wrong?"

Jack smiles. "If you let me stay, I'll forget it," I say.

"You are not good at blackmailing. Besides, there's nowhere you can stay."

"I could stay here," I say quietly. "Mo is your friend."

Jack says, "He has enough problems."

"You mean he wouldn't do it?"

"He does anything for me." Jack likes to boast about the friends he has and what they would do for him that not even his own flesh and blood would do.

"I could help out his mother, learn something from them."

"You don't give up easily, do you?"

If I had a daughter, then I would know exactly what's on her mind. But Jack doesn't have a clue about Mo. Why doesn't he stop and think, "Why does Tatum want to stay so desperately?" How could he know? They will never know.

"What doesn't she give up easily?" Mother wants to know.

Jack says, "Our bet. Tatum is convinced she will fail in economics. She wants to bet that if she wins, well, fails, she stays here a week longer."

"Hah." Mother's voice is full of sarcasm.

Jack says, "Well, why not?"

"I'll tell you when we're home," Mother says and gets in the car.

Jack looks at me, then at her, pretending that he is worried. I know he doesn't like it when she bosses him about, especially in front of other people. We get in the car and drive home. I look at the building for one last time before we drive away.

Yogurt

I wake up and think of Mother's black doll by the window in our house in London. Her eyes are white and her hair a wild bush. She is naked and sits with her legs crossed and her arms by her side, waiting. I think of the black doll once in a while and remember Mother saying, "She is my baby." She said she used to collect black dolls; anything she could find she would keep for her collection. Then, she said that one night, she dreamed that they had come to life and had tried to feed her baby food and she had said no, and they tried to suffocate her. The next day she had burned her dolls, all but the one by the window because that doll had stood by and not said anything.

The moon has already dissolved by the time I get out of bed heavy this morning. It feels like I have weights on my feet. My mouth is dry and my head is spinning. I want to cry.

Last night, I couldn't think of any stories of Mo that would have put me to sleep. I would wake up thinking I'm never going to see him again and he doesn't even know I love him.

Mother's voice is the loudest coming from downstairs. She says, "Yes," so loudly even the person in London would have to move the phone away from her ear. I come down the stairs feeling old, my skin stale from sleep and sweat. I don't even comb my hair because I want to know what all the noise is about.

"Shhh, what did you say?" Mother says, almost pushing Peter away from her. "Say it again. English, C; French, C; math, B; and physics, B? OK, now Mona."

Peter stares at the notes that he has written down while Mother says the results of our exams out loud.

"I got it. C, B, B, A. And Tatum?" she shouts down the phone. "Yeah? Yeah?"

I bite my fingernails thinking of Mo. Not that it would make a difference anyway.

Mother says, "A, A, A and B." She's talking to Mrs. Parsons, our next-door neighbor in London. "I'll tell them. OK. Thank you, darling. Bye."

Mother says, "Shirley sends her love and says congratulations."

"Let's celebrate," Jack turns to me and says. "And you lose the bet."

I go upstairs, wash my face, and put on my bathing suit and walk to the pool. I will not think of leaving. Think of now, your hands, body and feet. The water swims around me. I breathe after every stroke. My limbs move as I want them. I have control over my body; it does what I want it to do. Just breathe in and breathe out.

At the far end of the pool, I can see someone standing there. I stop swimming. Jack stands there grinning.

"When are you going to start packing?" he asks.

"Tonight. Why?" I say, holding on to the side of the pool.

"Do you want the good news or the bad news?"

"I don't care," I say. Something in his voice makes my heart beat fast.

"Bad news is your mother isn't talking to me now. And the good news is you have to pack," he says.

"Very funny," I say. I almost don't want to know what he has to say.

"To stay here," he says.

I stop beating my legs and just stare at him. All the blood has drained from me and then brought back. I don't know how to react. I don't want him to see that I'm so happy because of Mo, but to think that it's because of Africa. It's Africa I love. I keep saying to myself, "Don't let anything show."

"I talked to your dad and he said as long as the people you are staying with are like my family and all that. . . . You'll be staying with Mo."

I don't dare ask about Mum.

"I told your mother she should be proud of you and see this as a 'good notes' present." He turns to go.

"And Mo?" I ask.

"First, he said you would be uncomfortable there. He said he would come and check on you if you stayed at Mr. Porter's. But I said either with him or nothing."

"If he doesn't want me there," I say, "I don't want you to force him to let me stay."

"Mo's just a worrier. I told him it was good for you." The phone rings inside the house, and Jack walks back quickly.

Floating on my back, I watch the clouds and almost forget to breathe. I think of Mona and Mother and Peter and Dad and Jack, and I think of the black doll by the window.

When I go back to the house, I see Mother sitting by herself at the kitchen table. I don't know if I'm excited or scared. I watch her eat yogurt and dry bread. She likes that. She says it brings back childhood memories. It doesn't make sense since she said she had a sad childhood. I can't imagine Mother ever having a childhood; she doesn't have a single childhood photograph.

Now it's real. What am I going to do now? My crazy aunt walked away from our house asking the same thing. "What am I going to do now?" Her voice entered my head as she disappeared, like a song that would not leave. "What am I going to do now?"

For hours, I lie on the bed letting a slow sadness come to me. The room is cold. It reminds me of the time I woke up from the appendix operation and saw Mother standing over me. "Give me a comb. I want to comb my hair," I said to her. I don't dare go downstairs. When everyone has stopped making noises, I creep downstairs, take out the container from the fridge and some dry bread, and sit at the kitchen table and eat yogurt and dry bread. I wish I could ask Mother why she never called me her baby.

Light

The lemon yellow airport building looks different from when we first arrived. It's not as crowded as it was, and there is an echo above the mosaic tiles on the floor. The air is cool and fresh and the guards wear familiar, crisp, clean uniforms. Inside, everything is gray and dark blue and the only colors I see are the orange, yellow and red on women's scarves.

"I'll call every night," Mother says, looking over her shoulder as if the plane will lift off any minute. She says she always gets nervous when she's at airports, because she thinks she has done something wrong and she might be stopped. She says she gets stopped for body checks more often than other people, or they find fault with her passport or they want to check her suitcase. I think they get suspicious because she looks nervous.

"Salim will take care of everything," Jack says, hugging me. "Don't go anywhere alone; he will drive you."

Salim shakes hands with everyone. He hugs Mona and says that he will write or call. I hug Mona and kiss Peter's cheeks in the air like the French do. Mona looks sad. I don't mind saying good-bye because I know I'm going to see them again.

"You can do things your way," Jack says to me. "I know I can trust you. Any problems and Mo will help—he's just like a father."

When Mother, Jack, Mona and Peter pass through security, I think I see Mother crying but I don't know why. And then they're gone. I turn around and look at the bright sun outside and my heart sinks.

Salim drives, but it seems like eternity. Then I think of Dad. When I think of him, I think of not knowing. He is somewhere else and you don't know where because he doesn't tell you. Even when he was there, he wasn't really there. He made calls or had to go somewhere and meet someone or visit some friends. I never thought about missing him. Sometimes, I would imagine him there when he wasn't there, but then I couldn't think of anything I could say to him. The good thing about Dad's voice on the telephone was that I could give the phone to Mona or Peter or say I had to go when I didn't have anything else to say to him.

I drop off Ras, my chicken, at Mr. Porter's, so it could roam around in his garden.

I look at my watch and it's 6:30 P.M. I want to know exactly when Mo comes and goes, his habits, what day, what hour. I will notice his routine once I am there. When I used to come home from school, a man's coat hanging by the door meant that Dad was there. He would just appear from nowhere, and he would be sitting in the living room drinking tea. I would kiss him, and he would stay for a night, maybe two—I never knew. He wouldn't tell us when he was leaving. I would wake up one morning and call for him. "He's gone," Mother would say, like he had to just get up and leave. Grandma left me that way, too. She had pure white hair when she died. I came home from school, and everyone was crying. I was sad not because she was dead but because, just like Dad, she hadn't told me she was leaving.

The sunset is a purple haze on the horizon, and it gets wider as we drive. We reach Mo's house at twilight. A single drop of rain falls on the windscreen. One huge drop and then another falls and then another until there is enough of them to make a sound on the screen. By the time Salim stops the car, the rain is pounding like a million birds pecking at the car. I wait in the car and look up at Mo's window. The lights are on; the curtains are not drawn. Salim carries my suitcase up the stairs, and I follow him. The color of the staircase seems darker than before and smaller. Like Alice in Wonderland, things seem to change before my eyes. Mo's door seems smaller than the night we were here for dinner. Mo opens the door, says hello to Salim and me and takes my suitcase inside. Like a puppet, I follow his small shoulders to the spare room. I'm in a dream and I'm going to wake up and find myself in my room in London.

The strong smell of cloves and curry powder seeps out of the kitchen. I don't see his mother; maybe she is sleeping. I wonder if Mo has changed his furniture. Although I know they're the same tables and chairs, they just look older and more rigid now. Mo puts my suitcase on the bed in the spare room. The sheets are shiny white and the green armchair by the closet sits empty.

For a minute, I am ashamed and I wish I weren't here. I feel sorry for everyone. I want time to turn back and to be on the plane with Mona and Peter.

Mo opens the closet doors and shows me the hangers. I don't want him to see my face. I look out the window and watch the few cars driving by. Although the street looks almost empty, music and laughter fill the air. A woman holding a plastic bag is dancing on the sidewalk. She turns and turns, singing to herself.

"Fresh sheets are here." Mo points to the drawers beneath the closet. "The bathroom is on your left, and if you need anything, just knock on my door. My room is next to yours."

He leaves the room and I hear him talking to Salim in Swahili. My mind wanders to London and Mona. I am lonely. My suitcase sits there waiting for me. I shift the clothes around. Mo comes back in and says, "I go to work at eight and come back at six. Salim will take you wherever you want."

I just blurt out, "Shall I make you breakfast?" I'm not his wife. He looks at my suitcase and says, "My mother gets up at six and makes breakfast, lunch and dinner all in one. You don't have to do anything." He stands there looking at me, then he smiles.

I want to see him wake up, watch him move around the house, watch him eat and read and take a nap.

"Here's my work number. If you have any problems, just ask for Mohammad."

An hour later, dinner is on the table. His mother appears as we sit at the table. She serves us and then disappears.

I watch Mo eat slowly.

"Are you doing anything with Enzo tomorrow?"

"No, I'm going to stay here and write some cards," I say. I want to watch his mother cook, watch her hands and feet and see similarities.

"If you go out, try and get back before it gets dark." He wipes his thick mustache with his fingers. "If not, tell Salim to call and tell me where you are."

"OK."

I look over to him to see if he looks at me, but he just looks at his food. I want to know what he is thinking. He doesn't say much. He goes to the bathroom and I put the dishes in the sink. His mother motions to me that she wants to do the dishes. I go to my room and leave the door open.

There is a strange silence here. The noise coming from the kitchen, the water running in the sink and the sounds from the street make me homesick. The small bedside lamp makes my room look big and silent. I put on my sleeveless white nightdress and the same pink dressing gown Mother bought for me when I went to hospital to have my appendix out. I don't really want to wear the dressing gown, but the nightdress is thin and you can see through it. I put the dressing gown on and go into the kitchen. Mo is in his room. I must have missed him leaving the bathroom. I knock lightly on the bathroom to check if there is anyone in there.

The bright lamp in the bathroom is so strong it almost hurts my eyes. I look in the mirror and I think I can see wrinkles under my eyes. After I brush my teeth, I go past Mo's closed door and to my room. This is a big mistake. I don't want to be here.

Mastermind

Today I'm going to show him. I'm going to show him that I don't care. I will be calm and won't even look at him. The hours go by so slowly. What is Mona doing now? Is she sitting in her room thinking of Salim? In Mo's spare room, I sit there for hours, it seems, as if I'm in a coma. Then, the slow minutes that were sucked into a syringe inject life back into me when I know that he's going to come back tonight. I will wake up and I'll forget that I ever waited. I take a long bath and try to read the Hardy book in between the vapors. I let my hair dry slowly and crinkle it up with my fingers for the curls to look nice when he comes home. I cream my body slowly and push back the cuticles on my fingernails and cream my shriveled hands. I listen to the radio that his mother turns on in the morning and leaves on until she goes to bed at night. It plays African music all day.

I check my white, V-neck T-shirt in the mirror. If I bend down a little he can just see the roundness of my breasts. I put gloss on my lips and use the metal curler to curl my lashes. It's around 5:30 and he will be home soon. I help his mother set the table and bring the candle from the shelf in my room to light it up for dinner. And then I wait.

Exactly at six o'clock, he opens the door, and stands there looking at me. Something in the way he looks makes me feel like a woman. Then he turns and looks at the table that I have set and I'm locked out of his mind again.

"How pretty," he says, smiling. "A pretty table. Don't spoil us, because when you leave we'll miss you." I have to smile.

"It's nothing. Your mother did everything," I say. He goes to the bathroom to wash his hands.

I watch him at the table when we eat. What he does with his spoon or the way he holds the bread. I'm not really hungry. I bend over a little and reach for the bread. I watch him watch me.

"Did you go out?" he asks, biting off a piece of bread.

His mother doesn't leave the kitchen. I've never seen her eat.

"I was here," I say, putting a piece of bread in my mouth. "I wrote some cards and read something."

"So you relaxed."

"Yes."

"What did you do?" I ask.

"Work. Lifted boxes from one place to another."

"Maybe I'll come by tomorrow and say hi," I say.

"If you want."

We finish dinner while his mother makes noises in the kitchen with the radio on. Once in a while, she comes to the table to motion to Mo to eat more or motions for me to try something that I already ate when she was in the kitchen. Her movements remind me of a tree in the wind. Like a tree, she stands in one spot for a long time and just does things with her arms. After dinner, I go to my room and leave the door open. I hear sounds and try and imagine what Mo and his mother are doing.

Some time later, I smell coffee and walk to the kitchen. Mo sits at the table with his pajamas on, reading the paper, with a tiny coffee cup and a brandy glass.

"Do you want Turkish coffee?" He sips from the miniature cup.

I look into the cup, into the thick, dark liquid. He offers me the small cup. "Here, try some."

I sip a little and taste the bittersweet coffee. I wince.

He says, "Look at that face."

"It's strong." I feel him watching me. When he looks at me, he looks a little longer and smiles. I know I have won. I smile back and look down at the cup.

Suddenly it's so quiet I can hear crickets outside. His mother is nowhere in sight. I can smell the brandy on his breath from where I'm sitting. Somehow he sits differently, a little uncomfortable, like a shy, frightened boy. I feel strong, like those women in films who lie on beautiful beds with a long cigarette in their hands. He can't scare me anymore. Finally, I say what I've prepared in my head all day today, with all the right intonations. While I get up to go back to my room, I turn and say, "Can you play Mastermind?"

"What's that?"

"It's a little difficult." I say my rehearsed speech out loud. "Or do you want to play cards?"

"Let me finish reading the paper," he says, looking at the paper. "Then I'll play with you." I feel my heart beating faster, and I go into my room and take the pack of cards out of the top drawer. I put some gloss on my lips again, not too much, and look at myself in the mirror.

I hear him go to his room and I knock on the slightly open door.

"I haven't seen your room yet," I say. "Let's play here."

I practiced these simple words over and over in my head so he wouldn't think they meant anything. It's easy, because in my head, I just have to pretend that I am a fairy with wings and a magic wand and that I'm here to be kind to him. When I think of these things, my voice changes and I'm not nervous anymore. I am a harmless fairy.

"I'll get some fruit," he says. I sit on his bed with one leg beneath me and shuffle the cards.

He comes back with a plate and a knife and a bowl full of oranges, mangos, grapes and bananas.

"What are we playing?" he asks.

"Can you play poker?"

"The way you shuffle those cards, I don't think I want to play poker with you." He almost says the same thing I imagined he would say. Everything is going according to plan. He sits on the bed facing me and looks at the cards that I hand out quickly.

"We need money," I say.

"Change?"

"Anything."

We play some sets and it's obvious he doesn't know enough to play well.

"Your bets are too low," I say. "Take a risk. You can bluff, too."

"Maybe I was bluffing." He's concentrating on his cards.

"You'll learn." I win again and take his money.

"This isn't fair," he says. "You're stripping me of everything I have."

"I'll lend you some."

"No, I lose anyway."

"And I win."

He says, "Lucky at poker, unlucky in love. You know that, don't you?"

"So you are the lucky one in love?"

"No, I'm not lucky in either."

"I don't believe that."

"This one is mine. Full house, isn't it?" he asks.

I stare at his face and his body. He doesn't even look at me. Then he yawns.

"I have to go to sleep soon." He says, "Last round."

"Your last savings." I have a set of numbers. I put on a shy smile. I play the part of a fourteen-year-old girl. I want him to play his part, too.

I go to my room while he goes to the bathroom. I want him to touch me, but he has to do it. I can't force him to. I've thought it out and it has to happen. It seems like half an hour and he still isn't out of the bathroom. I lie on my bed with the door slightly open with the bedside lamp on. I lie on my side and pull the thin sheet over my face and practice crying. I think of the worst things that would make me cry. I think, How would I feel if Dad died? I don't feel much. Then I try with Mother and Jack and Peter. Then I force myself to think the same of Mona. I can't. She will never die. She will be here for me forever. I can't hold back the tears even thinking about it. I burst out crying and can't stop. I have to keep my voice down. But I can't help it anymore. I sob uncontrollably. I thought it was just practice but now it's for real. I don't know why I'm crying so hard and why I can't stop. It's as if I don't want Mo to come to my room anymore and I try and keep my voice down.

I feel a hand over my head and Mo pulls the sheet back a little.

He says softly, "What's the matter?"

I can't answer; I don't know what's wrong with me. He pulls the chair over and sits on the chair. I pull my legs up to my chest and cry a little louder.

"What's wrong?"

I manage to say, "I don't know."

"You don't like it here?"

"It's not that," I sniff. "I miss my family." I really think that I miss them.

He takes my hand and strokes it a little and strokes my wet hair from my face and hands me a tissue. His hand is so warm, I can feel it through my body.

"Do you want me to call them?"

"No," I say softly. "I just feel very lonely." My sobs get louder and louder and I just have to hold him. I move my head forward and put my head on his chest and cry. His body freezes. He doesn't touch me; he just says, "It's OK. It's all right."

He holds my shoulders and leads me back to my pillow. He tucks me in bed and turns off the light. "Good night. You'll feel better tomorrow."

My eyes are puffy from crying, and I don't look like a woman anymore. He closes the door behind him. I lie there biting my transparent nails and feel my heart beating fast. Mother isn't here to censor my dreams. She can't catch my thoughts and put them away in a closet and throw the key up to the stars. I dreamed that I was frightened and I was running. I was running and I cried while I ran. I cried in my bed, I cried on a train, I cried under my blanket until Mother came and stroked my hair the way she knows I like it until I fell back to sleep.

Time

This morning I woke up and wanted to peel away at my-self, but my hands kept on slipping. Like the baby I saw on TV inside its mother's stomach, all dark and watery, I kept on slipping. I am surrounded by a heap of silence. Mo must be asleep. I go to the bathroom with a magazine and sit on the side of the tub and I wait. I turn on the shower in the tub and let the water run. I sit there for a long time till I hear a noise in the kitchen. His mother won't come in the bathroom, because I haven't seen her use this bath-room before. I don't know where else she would go. I take off my nightdress and stand in the tub, pretending that Mo is in here watching me. I pull the shower curtain and let my body soak in the hot water. I don't turn the water tap on too high because it would be too loud and he would know I'm in here.

I wait under the stream of water and touch my breasts and hard nipples. I pull my fingers through my pubic hair and touch my thighs and feel goosebumps all over. I want him to come in. It seems like hours have gone past. I wait.

I pick up my toothbrush and brush my teeth so hard I don't hear him come in.

"Oh, God," he says and goes out saying, "I'm sorry."

I think of him standing there long enough to see my bare body behind the curtain. Did he see me touch my thighs?

I get out and wash out my mouth and put on the pink dressing gown with my hair still wet. He sits at the table drinking coffee. The smell smothers me. I look straight at him. "It was my fault. I forgot to lock the door."

He doesn't look at me. "I should have knocked. I'm sorry."

"No, it wasn't your fault." I even know what to say. After a while I say, "I'm going to the market today. Do you want to come?"

"I have to work."

"I'll bring you lunch, then."

"No, you don't have to."

"It's on my way."

"Are you feeling better this morning?"

"I'm sorry about last night," I say.

"You don't have to be sorry," he says, getting up and going to the bathroom. I clean up the table and go to my room. I like to sit on my bed and comb my hair slowly. It makes me feel all clean and white like a trim, hard doll. I hear the front door shut. He saw me in the shower. I sip the sweet, milky tea and think of the conversation we're going to have today. It's like making the future happen. It's like a prophecy. I think of things and what I'm going to say, then what he is going to say, and it happens.

Salim drives a straight line through the streets. He asks me how Mona is doing and says that he plans to go to London one day. It's hot outside and I am already sweating. I wish Mona were here now. She would tell me where to go and what to do. Like a heavy brick, Mona's picture sits in my head every time I feel lonely.

There aren't many traffic signs on the roads. People walk anywhere, even in the middle of the street. It must be difficult for Salim to concentrate because of all the people and the colors. He stops by the Kariakoo market to drop me off. He says he'll be back in two hours. I turn the corner expecting the warehouse not to be there, but it's still there. I walk around, looking at the market stalls, pretending I'm being watched. Maybe Mo is filming me and I don't know it. Maybe he will play it back when I'm gone and he might get sad because he never touched me. But he doesn't have a TV.

Maybe I'll buy his mother some flowers. I walk around aimlessly, waiting for time to pass. In an hour, I will go over and take him his lunch. I buy some nuts and some coconut juice. At a jewelry store, I choose a ring with a flower motif on it. The leaves are yellow and the center is painted black. There is a matching necklace but the center is white, so I don't buy it.

At around 12:30, I walk toward the warehouse and open the metal doors. There's no one around and I can't hear any sounds. I'm so nervous; it feels like I have demon jellyfish swimming in my stomach. After a few minutes, a side door to the building opens and a man with one arm comes out. He stares at me.

"Is Mohammad here?"

He turns and shouts into the building, "Mohammad!" and walks away as if that's his job around here. He disappears behind some boxes. I hear Mo's footsteps come from far away. As the footsteps get louder, I take out the sandwich I have made for him. On either side are boxes and boxes of all sizes. Some are new cardboard, and some are so tattered you wonder if they can hold anything in them.

"Sandwiches," I say, holding out the bag.

"Thank you." He takes the bag with his grubby hands. "Nice ring."

I look at my hand. "Thanks."

He says, "Did you come on your own?"

"Yes," I say. "No, Salim is picking me up again."

He looks around at the silence and then says, "So, I'll see you tonight." He holds the bag up and says, "Thank you." We both turn and walk opposite ways. I listen to his footsteps getting softer until I don't hear them anymore.

Salim is already there when I go back. I get in the car and go back to the flat. He asks some more questions about Mona. It's really hard to concentrate on giving him answers.

Back at the flat, I lie on my bed and close my eyes, thinking of nothing in particular. I feel like a sponge, totally empty until a thought, like a worm, bores through me until it gets bigger and bigger.

I write a letter to Mona telling her how much I miss her and how much I can't wait to see her next week. I tell her that Salim asks about her every time he sees me. I ask her all sorts of questions, which is stupid because I know she's not going to be answering them anyway. I wear my jeans and a black top and I wait. I want to see Mo before Enzo comes to pick me up for dinner tonight. I'm surprised Enzo is allowed to drive, but I guess nobody here cares about underage driving.

Finally, Mo comes home. His voice is the only voice I hear, uninterrupted by his mother's silence. I leave my room and go to the kitchen.

"I got something for you," he says, handing me a little packet.

He has bought me something. So he did think of me today.

I say thank you and open the box. The necklace is a flower just like my ring but with a white dot in the middle.

"I was going to buy this today," I say. I'm so happy I don't know what else to say.

"I'm glad you like it."

I go to the bathroom and put it on. I want to wear it tonight. I go over to him and give him a quick peck on the cheek. I can smell his face. His day-old scaly beard scratches my face.

"I hope you report all this to Jack so that he knows I'm taking good care of you."

Enzo blows the car horn outside and I say bye and leave with crumbling butterflies in my stomach.

I TURN THE KEY SLOWLY, trying not to make too much noise to wake Mo's mother. The evening with Enzo felt like forever. I can't even remember what we talked about; my mind was home with Mo. When I go in, I see that the light in the hallway has been left on for me. His door is slightly open. I hear his deep breathing. He's probably asleep. I go to my room and undress and read the rest of Hardy in bed. My eyes are tired and I think I fall into a light sleep, because a noise wakes me up. There's someone in the bathroom. I must have dozed off. I pull the cover off me and cover only my foot and parts of calves with the sheet. Lying on my side, my thighs shine in the faint light coming from the bathroom. The thought of Mo seeing me like this excites me. I hear the bathroom door unlock. Then I pretend that I'm asleep. I don't move and keep my eyes half-shut. His muffled footsteps stop in front of my door. I hear him pick up my blanket from the chair, and cover me with it. He turns the light off, leaves the room and closes the door behind him. In the silence of the room and the gravelike darkness, he saw my thighs.

Jump

Wine tastes like vinegar and sugar. It's bitter and I drink it because it makes me feel happy. At the restaurant, Mo said next time I order something, it's going to be Coke or nothing. He looked like he had committed a crime and had to undo it. He said he didn't want the responsibility on his hands.

When we came back, I told him, "You're the nicest man I know." And he said, "Sleep well."

Now, in my room I think I can smile forever. My head feels heavy and my nipples are getting hard. I know he likes me. I can feel it when he looks at me. He looks at me differently. I think I saw the guilt on his face. I know I have something that he doesn't. I can't say exactly what it is, but I have it.

I get out of bed and put on my dressing gown and my slippers. My head is giddy from the wine. I can't sleep. I pace the room and thoughts race through my head. It's all so fast and hazy. Mo is probably lying down on his bed reading the paper. It's so quiet I can hear myself breathing short, quick breaths.

Scene after scene goes by in my head and I can't breathe. I have to get out of the room. I put on the flower necklace he bought for me and go to the kitchen, and for a moment I can hear him in his room. It will just take one second. I have to do it now. I'm scared, just like when I was at the top of the ten-foot diving board in London. I was standing at the top, and I knew if I just jumped, it would all be over. I wouldn't die. I looked down and my body froze. I imagined myself jumping but I couldn't. "Jump, jump," I told myself, but a glass wall was holding me back. So I went back down the steps and thought I'll do it some other day.

Now I can't move. I imagine myself knocking and going in but my body doesn't move. It's frozen and I don't know what to do.

I see the walls spinning around me. I will never drink alcohol again. I take a deep breath and knock on Mo's door. The sound of it wakens me from my thoughts. I can't show that I'm scared. I push the door a little and see Mo lying on his bed reading a book.

"Yes?" his voice asks from behind the door.

"Can you help me take this off?" My voice is so weak, I think he can't hear me.

There is silence and he doesn't respond.

I walk toward his bed, walking as straight as I can. He puts his book down and sits up. Turning my back to him, I kneel so that he can take my necklace off. My head is so hot I think it will explode.

"There," he says.

I turn and kneel in front of him. I can't look at his face. I feel so ashamed.

I say, "Thank you." I sit there frozen.

He says, "What kind of game are you playing?"

"What do you mean?" I keep a straight face.

"Whatever it is, you are just a young girl."

For one second I look at his confused face and I know. He looks down somewhere at the bedsheets and his face is so pitiful, I want to share his loneliness with him.

"I've seen the way you look at me," I say.

"What?" I want to hold his head on my chest and kiss his hair.

"When we danced, I felt you . . ."—I can't say it loud, but I have to say it, say it and get it over with—". . . get hard." Like a dog that has a piece of gristle stuck in his throat, Mo looks like he's in pain.

I take his hand in mine and he doesn't move. He just looks at my hand and his as if they were someone else's. I bring his hand up to my lips and kiss his long and strong fingers and rub his hand against my face. He just sits there looking at his knees.

"I'm a woman. Everyone says I look twenty." I want to press his hand against my neck but he pulls back.

"You fantasize about me, don't you?" I lean over to his face expecting to be pushed away. I kiss his lips and his mustache. He does not respond. He just sits there. I know he can feel my breathing because it's so loud I think it will wake his mother. I kiss his mouth again and his cheeks.

"I dreamed about you one night," he whispers. Mo's face takes on a look of concentration that I have never seen before. His forehead creases heavily as if in each ridge he is hiding humiliation and disgrace. It isn't his face anymore.

He moves his face toward me without moving the rest of his body. Then I see his lips move and he kisses me. I am so shocked I don't know what to do. He kisses my lips slowly and then my cheek and my forehead. I am in heaven. My body is pulsating. He looks like he's struggling with something. Mo stares at me like he's seeing a woman from another time.

"Mo," I say instinctively. As if this is some sign that he has been waiting for. He holds my shoulders and rubs my arms like he's making a pottery figure with his hands. Then he pulls me down to the bed. I catch myself in the mirror on the wall, and I think I'm beautiful.

He's doing this for me. It's wrong and I am his friend's daughter, but he is doing it for me.

What if his mother walks in? I don't know what to do now. I think I have lost control. I don't know what he is going to do to me. I lie on the bed and can't look at him. I am scared. My heart is beating fast. He kisses my neck just like women are kissed on TV. His hand comes down slowly and touches my left breast. He squeezes it and it hurts. Then he takes my left hand and raises it above my head on the pillow. He holds it so I can't move. I don't know what to do. I can't tell him to let go. He touches my hips and my thighs with his right hand and I lie there feeling everything. It feels like I'm outside my body and watching him. My body tingles. I just try to breathe. I want to move my left hand but his squeezes it harder and pushes it on the pillow. Now I know what it feels like to be paralyzed and not be able to tell your hand or your leg to move. His right hand moves inside my inner thigh and I hear myself moaning. It can't be me. This is not my body and this is not my warmth. Then he pushes back my robe and pulls down my pajama pants a little while he searches for the panty line. His face comes down to mine and he bites my lower lip. His hard hand is inside my panties and he starts rubbing me. My moan is so loud I am embarrassed. It feels like magic. He touches me there—the same place that I touch myself at night when I think of him. But it's not the same. It's different. It's better. I don't want him to stop. I put my right hand on his hand and feel it there on me and I think I am dreaming. I want him to touch me a little higher and a little faster. I press hard on his hand and my body wiggles like a snake. Suddenly I realize he has his tongue in my mouth and I didn't even notice it. He moves his tongue around. It's hard and warm. I don't know what to do with it so I touch it slightly with the tip of my tongue. Then I taste it. I want to taste its flavor and keep it in me. His hand moves a little faster and I forget his mouth again. His hand is so gentle I press harder on it and say, "Mo." I can't stop myself. I can't control myself. I hear myself saying, "Yes," over and over again and as if my other self has risen out of my body and has gone somewhere else. I'm not me, just a body that I can't control. The feeling starts in my thighs and moves between my legs and tickles and then aches. The feeling is so familiar but so different. I want to tell him not to stop and he rubs me over and over until my gasp makes him rub me even more.

For one second I open my eyes and look at him. I see him staring at my face and he looks like a man in pain. He has the look of desperation on his face. As if he is lost in hell and can't find his way out. He looks at me and says, "You're beautiful." My heart sinks, because now I know it. I know I am strong and he has lost control.

I close my eyes and feel the surge of sun in me and I stop breathing. It is so strong that it almost hurts, and when it's all over, I close my legs and keep his hands there between my thighs. He puts his head on my chest and I realize all along he was not even on the bed. He had been kneeling beside the bed all the time fully dressed. His head doesn't move from my chest. The more I look at him, the more he begins to look like bits and pieces of shadows. His head drops, heavy with flaws. He looks worn-out with disgust. He just gets up and goes into the bathroom. I lie there not knowing what to do. I don't know what to say. In my fantasies at night in my bed it never got this far. I couldn't think of such a scene, so I left it out. Now I'm here without a script and I don't know what to do.

I cover my face with my hands. They smell of Mo.

Secrets

When I was younger, I used to make up stories the night before I went to school. I would gather some girls around me in the courtyard and tell them stories about all sorts of things. Once, I told them that a man came to our house when no one was home. He took off my bra and took off my panties. Then he hid them and I had to go look for them. I looked under the table, and they weren't there. I opened the drawers and they weren't there. Finally, I had to come to school without my panties. All I had to do was close my eyes at night and make up stories and bring them to school the next day. All the girls had to do was listen and believe me. "But you don't even wear a bra," one of the girls said. The other girls laughed. My stories were mine and they belonged to me and they could either believe me or not.

Last night, Mo went to the bathroom and didn't come out for a long time. I got up and went to my room, pulled the covers over my face and cried. There was no other noise. I cried in an empty church once. I had gone inside to get away from the rain. There was no one there. I could hear the pigeons flapping their wings above and I could hear tapping on the empty wooden benches and I could hear the wind around the golden candlesticks. I thought I was the only person left in the world. Everyone had died and the church was my shield. My heels split the silence. When the pigeons flew away, I cried.

Mo couldn't hear me. When I got up this morning, he had already gone to work. I had a shower and stood under the water for a long time. Then I got dressed, called Salim and got him to drive along the ocean toward Bahari Beach. I didn't want to get out. I looked out the window at the ocean through the glass that kept me in.

Now I'm weak and tired and I want to go home to London. I don't want to go back to Mo's house.

Salim drops me in front of the flat and drives away. I don't want to go in. I want to go to my room without seeing him. It's only early afternoon and he'll be coming in a few hours. It's as if I'm in a trance. I can't think. This must be what it feels like to sleepwalk. Time goes by slowly and I sit there staring out the window listening to the noises his mother makes in the kitchen.

My heart drops when I hear the key in the door. I get up and quickly pretend I'm doing something in the closet. I hear him go to his room and close the door. He doesn't come out for some time. Then I hear a soft knock and I'm still standing before my closet. He comes in.

"How was shopping?" Mo has a basketful of coconuts in one hand and a bag of rice in the other. He looks old and tired.

"How did you know?" I say shyly.

"I called, and my mother said you had gone out."

"How was your day?" I ask with a little smile. This time the smile is the one I would use for Jack or Dad when I want something. I say, "I called my parents." Mo looks like he is someone else. He's not Mo; he's playing someone else's life. "I told them I was fine and that you said hi."

"What did Jack say?" he asks.

"He said hi back."

He looks so weak and drained. He turns and goes to his room and I don't hear anything from his room.

Then I hear the front door and I go to see if he's leaving.

He turns and says, "I'm going for a walk." I had planned our conversation in my head all day. I never imagined he would act like this. He is the adult; he's not supposed to leave me here and show that he's guilty and weak.

"Can I come with you?" I ask him.

He nods and goes out the door. I follow him. We walk a little in the streets until we reach the beach and walk on the sand. The sand smells of old soil. I take off my shoes; he leaves his shoes on.

"Did I do something wrong?"

"No," he says. "Why would you?"

He looks puzzled, almost annoyed. I wish I could tell him that I dreamed about him night and day for so long and that now, he's too real and my dreams were better. Mo's face is flushed from anger or embarrassment or just the walk.

Mo stops, holds my shoulders and for a moment, I think he's going to kiss me. "I don't know what's going on in your head," he says.

"Do you mean last night?"

"What do you mean?" Does he not remember last night? I don't want to be the first to talk about it.

"You like to play games?" Mo begins walking. "You walk around half-naked; maybe that's the way you've been brought up. Your shirt buttons are undone; you sleep without covers; you leave the bathroom door open; you want me to be ashamed?" I don't know how to react. I hadn't prepared for this. "Look, you're smart, you speak three languages, you keep on asking me questions, you're sweet, but you're fourteen. I want to be left alone. Do you understand?"

"I'm sorry," I say with a young voice. Maybe he likes it that way. Maybe he thinks I'm moping. Mo doesn't even mention our kiss—as if it never happened.

I think back to the black-and-white picture I keep in my drawer. The one where our family is sitting together at a table. I must have been five years old and I have a short, pretty white dress on. I have a little handbag with its handle in my mouth and I am sitting on a young man's lap. It's Dad. He has both arms around my shoulders and he's looking at the camera. That's the picture I like most. When I think of Dad, I think of a white dot far away in the sky. Sometimes, when I'm fading into sleep, I imagine him coming to my bed and covering my thighs with a blanket. Then I think of the picture of Dad's friend with his arms around me. He touched my breasts in the ocean. He knew I wouldn't scream if he did. He knew I was pretending to be a little girl. He knew I wasn't shy.

I don't need any photos or diaries or even belongings here; I have my memories. They're all fixed in my mind and I can call up anything I want and change and re-arrange it the way I want to.

Tea and Toast

I thought I saw his folding shadow at the door last night. I waited and I don't remember if I slept. Maybe Mo lies in bed at night and can't sleep, too. He doesn't want me here.

Maybe it's the heat or the bed or the steel darkness; it's only at night that I feel different. I lie on the bed at night and look at the ceiling and can't fall asleep. I look at him in the morning and I don't feel anything. It's not my body; it's someone else's at night. If I dyed my hair blond and came out of my room the next morning, would I be the same person?

His mother clatters about in the kitchen. The street outside is already noisy and dusty. And the radio plays "If You Ring My Bell." If I could make time stand still, then it would be this moment. I would sit at the table drinking tea with both of them frozen like two pieces of jewelry. I have gotten used to the tea, the boiled milk and sugar and tea and herbs. It's strong, sweet, bitter and milky. Will I drink this tea in London to remember him? Will I eat dry bread and yogurt at night when Mother dies?

Mo is sitting in the kitchen with his back to me. He looks like an old workman I saw at the airport in Spain. The man was sitting by the side of the road having his lunch. Maybe he had never been anywhere. He looked up at planes and maybe wished he were in one of them. But where would he go? What about his children and his mother?

I could stop everything this moment, pack my bags and leave as if nothing ever happened, as if I never said anything.

"Do you want tea?" Mo asks. He is sipping his tea.

"Yes, please."

"Sit down. I'll make some toast." I sit down. I don't want to watch him get up. I don't like the way he moves. He pours me some tea and gets me toast. His fingers are brown and thick, and the skin on his hand looks like old lizard skin.

"Have you eaten?" I ask him.

A dog barks in the street below. Barks all sound the same to me. Mo says, "Yes," as he gets up to clear the table. "When is your flight?"

"Friday," I say. Mo's moves are like a man who has a heavy cloak on his shoulders and he can't get it off. Maybe I'll dye my hair tonight.

"I won't disturb you," I say. I imagine him standing at the door and telling me to leave.

"Just be yourself, Tatum," he mumbles. He smells of sleep. I don't feel anything.

Still I can't do anything. I can't choose; either I stay here until Friday or I go to Mr. Porter's. Helplessness creeps up to me.

He washes the dishes carefully. This is his home and it's his Africa.

The Telephone

Mr. Porter's house is the twin version of our house, only everything is the other way round. I'm reading the last chapters of Hardy while Enzo plays some silly game around the pool chasing Ras, my chicken. Mr. Porter is looking after Ras until Enzo leaves. Enzo must be an orphan because I have never heard him talk about his parents. I can't imagine what they look like or how old they might be. I'm sure he wants to be a good-looking teenager who's so cool that girls fall in love with him. But then again, he listens to classical music and loves to play golf. I like his humor, though.

"Stay here till tomorrow," Enzo says. "It's cramped in that flat."

There is one single palm tree in Mr. Porter's garden. It is so tall you have to be lying down, like I am now, to see the top of it.

"Jack might call there," I say. "Mo is his friend," as if that's going to make the flat bigger.

The grass is cut short and it has some yellow patches. Otherwise there isn't much else here. Two short bushes with cones of tiny red flowers on either side of the pool. I don't like red flowers—especially not these ones. Red makes them look like they will burst open their insides and scatter their pollen in the air. It makes me want to take in deep fresh breaths when I look at red. The only perfect flower in the world is the sunflower. It's big and round and perfect and the insides are compact— no pollen to fly around in the wind. If a blind man asks me to let him feel a flower, it would be a sunflower.

"Call Jack from here," Mr. Porter says. He hands me lemonade he has made himself. "Tell him you'll be here. I'll take you to the airport." Mr. Porter has already dialed the number and says, "Hey, Jack, this is your neighbor and I have taken your daughter hostage." Then he laughs into the phone. He gives me the phone. "Here, he wants to talk to you."

Jack wants to know if I'm having fun and how my chick is doing. He asked me the same question yesterday. I tell him everything is great and that Mr. Porter and Enzo say I should stay for the last night. He wants to know about Mo and I tell him that he has been very kind.

"A few rules around this house," Mr. Porter says after I hang up. "This house is your house. No one goes hungry here, and don't be shy to ask for anything." Mr. Porter keeps one set of jingling keys in his right pocket warning everyone of his arrival, and probably has locks on everything he owns.

I call Mo and tell him that I'm staying here tonight. He says OK. He says, "Take care," and hangs up.

Enzo is fun sometimes. He plays the violin. He brought it out and played something from Bach and I loved it. He thinks that I'm homesick so I tell him that I miss London. "You'll be there soon. I have to stay here." He plays another song for me.

"You're out of it today," Enzo says.

"It's the weather."

"Let's go to Wimpy's." Although it's not really Wimpy's, the sign says Wimpy's. They have hamburgers and a lot of chips. I call Mo from the phonebox before we go in and no one picks up the phone. I wonder where he is. I know that he doesn't work on Sundays.

"Can I ask you something?" Enzo asks.

"Why do people ask that?" I say.

"What?"

"Why can't you just ask? Why do you have to ask to ask?"

"Never mind," Enzo says.

I can't stay at Mr. Porter's; I want to go back to Mo's tonight. I order chips and a chocolate sundae for dessert and I feel a little better.

Enzo drives to a sort of fun fair that is in the middle of nowhere. There is nothing on either side. The fair looks as if it's been put together in a hurry and it's just about to leave. Everywhere I go I expect to see Mo. We get on to a cup and saucer thing that moves round and round slowly. Everything looks so small. Where did all this come from?

The air has cooled slightly and the night air strokes my shoulders. The sky has the same color as the sky in winter at home, and if I didn't know I was in Africa, I would think it was going to snow.

"Would you tell anyone you loved them?" I ask Enzo.

"Of course I would."

"How would you know, though?" I say.

"It's a feeling."

"But what if you feel it one day and the next day it's gone?" I ask.

"Then it's not love. It's attraction." Enzo talks like a grown-up. Then he asks, "Why did you stay?" He looks embarrassed.

219

"I don't know," I say. "What do you think?"

"I don't know," he says. "What's Mo like?"

Maybe he knows.

"What do you mean?" I ask.

"I mean, he's a nice guy, right?" he asks.

"Yes, he's nice," I say.

"He could be the perfect father," he says.

"Maybe."

We stop and look at the stars. When I'm in London, Dar es Salaam is going to be the other planet. This thought calms me and I smile to myself.

"Have you French-kissed before?" Enzo asks.

I don't show any reaction. "Of course I have."

He says, "How about . . . you know?"

"No," I say.

"Come on."

"It's the truth," I say.

"Sure."

"I'm only fourteen."

"So?"

"Have you?" I ask.

"Yes."

"How often?"

"How often with one person or how many?"

"How many?"

"One," he says. "How many did you think?"

"More than one."

Then he says quickly, "Can I kiss you?"

"No."

"Why?"

"Because I don't want you to," I say.

"Are you staying with us tonight?" He pretends as if nothing has happened.

"I don't know." Maybe I *should* have kissed him.

When we go in the house, Enzo goes straight to the fridge, just like Jack, and stands in front of it and stares at the food inside.

"When are you going back?" I ask.

"Two weeks."

I say, "Are you excited?"

"Yeah. It gets boring here."

"I think I want to come back sometime."

"It's nothing special."

"I love it." I don't know that I do.

"Places are special when there are special people there." He sounds like Mother. She takes something that has happened and makes a general statement out of it. And everyone thinks it's a famous saying by somebody.

I want to see Mo and tell him that I'm not angry with him. I sit on Mr. Porter's sofa thinking about calling him. The phone rings and Enzo says that it's for me. I say, "Hello," but it's only Mother. She wants to know if I miss them and I say yes, and whether I regret having stayed and I say no. Mona says she misses me and asks how Salim and my chick are doing. I tell her I miss her, too.

Mr. Porter comes in and wants to know if we had fun. Then I ask him if he minds if I go back tonight. Something like I have to pack and buy some stuff tomorrow.

"If you leave, we'll keep your chicken as hostage," he says. Enzo doesn't say anything. I get my things and Enzo drops me off at the mattress shop.

Penda

His mother opens the door. This time I want to remember what she is wearing.

"He sleep," she says and lets me in.

I wonder what her first thoughts are when she wakes up in the morning. Why she chooses to wear one flowery red, purple and white blouse instead of another. If she, at one time, had ambitions. Or did she just wake up one day and say, I want to cook for my son till I die?

I go to my room and unpack my bag. I can't hear anything next door. It's dark and quiet here. Outside, the moon lights up the uneven street. Shirtless men ride their bicycles loaded with rumpled bags. Their arched backs glow as they ride back home all used up. There is sadness here; I don't know if it's the street or the shadows in the street. I want the moon to be there when I go back.

On the way to the bathroom, I see that his door is slightly ajar. The light from the window shines on his half-covered body. I walk in slow motion. I just want to watch him sleep. I lock the door behind me. His room smells stuffy.

I kneel by the bed and watch him sleep. His lips beneath the gray-black mustache look thinner than before. The frown lines on his forehead make him look uneasy. In the round, dark space of his face, Mo looks undignified. I stretch my hand out a little and touch his warm hand. His steady, deep breathing tells me I can touch him a little more.

I want to kiss his dark purple lips. Taste the mustache in my mouth. I lean over slowly and just brush my lips against his. His face twitches a little as if to shoo a fly.

He opens his eyes and stares at me as if he wasn't sleeping. I kiss him again and he doesn't move.

I say, "What do you think of me?"

"Is it important?" he says.

"I want to know." I want him to say he loves me.

After a long time, he says, "I think you are pretty and bright."

"Do you love me?" I ask him.

He stares at me for so long, I think he has turned to stone. Then he says in a commanding voice, "Take off your clothes."

"What?" I smile nervously.

"Take your clothes off." His tone is louder.

I want to cry. How could he? He hates me. I'm so stupid.

"You want to know what it's like?" he says and holds my wrist. I want to pull away and he holds so tight it hurts.

He kisses me hard on the lips and then draws back. For the first time he looks ugly and mean.

"It's not as nice as you think," he says as if he is acting on stage. He is playing another game and I'm not prepared.

If this was a film, what would the girl do? Would she run out of the room crying? In my version of the film, the girl stays because she is curious. I don't want him to know that he's hurting me. I don't want him to see me cry.

I say, "Show me." All the while my heart is beating faster and I want to run but something is holding me there. I want to stay.

He says, "No."

"You won't hurt me," I say.

I go toward him and open the first two buttons of my blouse. He looks at me. I take his hand and bring it to my face. I kiss his hands and fingers and bring it to my blouse buttons.

He opens the buttons quickly as if he has done this in his sleep. He pulls down my blouse and looks at my breasts. I think I see him licking his lips. Then he brings his hand up to caress my hair. His hand slides down to the bottom of my hair and he suddenly pulls it. It hurts. He kisses my neck and it's as if the pain isn't there anymore. He pulls back my hair and bites me. I want to push him away and tell him that he's hurting me. But it's nice.

It's as if I'm flying. I'm not really there. I'm floating. My insides hurt and in between my thighs I feel wet. I hold my breath when he touches my breast. He touches it so lightly and then brings his head down and kisses my nipples. Then he bites them and it hurts. He pushes me onto the bed and pulls down my panties. My body is excited and I wait to see what he's going to do. He takes off his pants and his underwear and his penis stands erect. I have never seen a real one before. I saw them in pictures we used to sneak into school and I thought how ugly they looked, like the ones on donkeys and horses, just smaller. Even seeing animals mounting each other on TV frightens me. Mo's looks ugly and big. It's scary. I don't want him. I want to get away. He lies on top of me and spreads open my legs and touches me down there. All I can think

224

of is, I don't want to get pregnant. Ella and I have the horrors when we think of men and how they can make us pregnant. Then we wouldn't be able to go to school or to parties. The thought of a baby makes me stiffen up. I can't breathe because I don't want him inside me. It's going to hurt. He slowly pushes himself in and my face tells him that it hurts. He doesn't push; he just stays there and breathes in and out. He looks flushed. It stings down there and I want to push him away but I want him to stay on top of me. I think of curved white sails on the ocean, veiled women, ancient ruins and colorful spices. He moves his hips just a little and again and then again. He looks at me. "Does it hurt?" I nod and he wants to come out but I hold him down on me. He moves slowly and then a little quicker and then his body moves on its own until he moans and then it's over.

I don't want to look at his body. It's sweaty and hairy. I look away. I want to get up and go to my room but maybe he'll get upset. I want him to tell me to go to my room.

He says, "Are you another person now?"

"Yes," I say although I don't feel it. I just feel sleepy.

"You have a beautiful body."

"*Penda.*"

"What?"

"It means love," I say.

"I know," he says. Then he says, "Are you glad to go back?"

I pretend to think although I knew it the moment he was inside me. "Yes."

"I'm sorry," he says.

"Thank you." My mind is elsewhere. I don't know what else to say.

It wasn't like my dreams.

"What is it?"

I say, "This is like a dream."

"Bad or good?"

I say, "Both."

There is a long silence. Then I think tomorrow I won't be here anymore. Am I going to think back to this place ever?

"Will you take me to the airport?" I ask.

Blue Blanket

I tried to die today.

This morning, Mo came into my room to get my suit-cases. I tried to kiss him on the lips. He pushed me away. "What do you think you're doing?" I mumbled something like "Last night was nice. I thought . . ." He looked at me in a strange way. "What are you talking about, Tatum?" Then I started to cry.

"Why are you acting like this?" he asked. "What do you mean last night?" Maybe he was just playing games. Maybe he was ashamed and wanted to pretend nothing happened. I remember I was confused. What if I dreamed it all and it never happened? I remember I moved automatically and followed Mo to the car. I remember that my body was numb and lifeless; this was happening to someone else. It's not me who's going back. And I remember I couldn't smell anything and I couldn't feel my tongue in my mouth.

On the plane, I closed my eyes and thought and thought where to put Mo's picture in my head so I would never see it again. So I put it in a casket, with myself inside, nailed it shut and pushed it off the edge of the world. As the casket fell, I opened my mouth, and my aunt, Dad's friend, mangos, coconuts and blood, Peter's left leg, Jack's belly, milky tea, fever, yellow chicks, blue shame and God flew out. I opened my eyes and saw myself sitting with emptiness on the plane next to a man who looked a little like Dad.

Why doesn't the ocean move when you fly over it? It's like a block of glassy blue mirror that lets ships glide all over it.

Mo hugged me. I remember the hug.

I'll remember the shadows on the ceiling when Mo was inside me.

I have a bruise on my right thigh. I don't know where I bumped myself, maybe while Mo was in between my thighs. It's his bruise. It simply appeared on its own accord. It's growing and I can't do anything about it. But every day when I look at it, it'll get smaller and fade into shades of yellow until, one day, I'll wonder whatever happened to it. I'll think of Mo and think he was never there.

What if Dad knew?

What if he knew I made love to a man called Mo?

What if he knew it was somebody else and not really me?

My crazy aunt told me she could hear leaves talk. She said they spoke to her about the beginning and the end of the world. She told me about a woman who was banished to the moon because her tongue was violent. The woman walked around the surface of the moon and listened to stories from heaven. My aunt pointed to the moon one night and said, "See there. There she is. Do you see her?" I looked up and thought I saw her before Mother pulled me away into the kitchen. "Don't tell her lies, do you understand?" My aunt, rubbing her lips hard until they were strawberry red, looked lovingly at Mother and said, "Oh, honey, I have so much liquid in me."

The man next to me says, "*Jambo.*"

I pull the blue blanket up to my neck and say, "Hello."

Africa looks so bruised and small from here.

I think of the pillow that slipped and fell to the floor when Mo pushed himself inside.

For a minute, I feel full and colorful in my stomach.

I can feel only my lips, my tongue, swollen and warm in my mouth.

Maybe somebody else told this story and it wasn't me. But I won't tell.